'He looks great.' Eden smiled fondly, because Ben did. Out of the hospital pyjamas and dressed in *real* clothes he looked just like any other little toddler, clutching a soft toy and dozing in his car-seat.

'So do you!' And there was nothing light or flip about Nick's voice. His statement was delivered in a low, husky voice, and Eden jerked her head to face him. Even with the barrier of his shades, she could feel the admiration in his gaze. 'You look stunning, Eden.'

'It won't last.' Somehow it was Eden who managed light and flip. 'My mum bought me some hair straighteners, but despite the promises I doubt they're quite up to a warm, humid Sydney Christmas.' She was babbling—terribly so—wishing Nick would just tear his eyes away, wishing he would start the engine so that she could remember how to breathe again. 'Nick…'

Carol Marinelli recently filled in a form where she was asked for her job title and was thrilled, after all these years, to be able to put down her answer as writer. Then it asked what Carol did for relaxation and after chewing her pen for a moment Carol put down the truth—writing. The third question asked—what are your hobbies? Well, not wanting to look obsessed or, worse still, boring, she crossed the fingers on her free hand and answered swimming and tennis, but, given that the chlorine in the pool does terrible things to her highlights and the closest she's got to a tennis racket in the last couple of years is watching the Australian Open—I'm sure you can guess the real answer!

Recent titles by the same author:

Mills & Boon® Medical Romance™
EMERGENCY: A MARRIAGE WORTH
   KEEPING *(A&E Drama)*
UNDERCOVER AT CITY HOSPITAL
(Police Surgeons)
SPANISH DOCTOR, PREGNANT NURSE
(Mediterranean Doctors)

Carol also writes for Modern Romance™.

Mills & Boon® Modern Romance™
HIS PREGNANT MISTRESS *(Expecting!)*
IN THE RICH MAN'S WORLD
(For Love or Money)

CHRISTMAS ON THE CHILDREN'S WARD

BY
CAROL MARINELLI

MILLS & BOON®

First published in Great Britain 2005
Large Print edition 2006
Harlequin Mills & Boon Limited,
Eton House, 18-24 Paradise Road,
Richmond, Surrey TW9 1SR

© The SAL Marinelli Family Trust 2005

ISBN 0 263 18872 8

Set in Times Roman 17 on 19¼ pt.
17-0606-50522

Printed and bound in Great Britain
by Antony Rowe Ltd, Chippenham, Wiltshire

CHAPTER ONE

'HEY!'

Coming out of his office, chatting away to a rather pretty, rather blonde physiotherapist, Consultant Paediatrician Nick Watson was flattened against the wall as Eden Hadley rushed past, visibly upset.

Visibly, because Eden was incapable of hiding her emotions. Along with wearing her heart on her sleeve, her expressive face told anyone who cared to look exactly what she was thinking, and right now it didn't take a degree in psychology to work out that she was far from happy. Her pretty full mouth was set in a grim line and her dark brown eyes flashed angrily as Nick caught her arm to halt her progress. Her long, dark, chocolate curls fell out of her loose ponytail as she swung around to confront him.

'Just leave it, Nick,' Eden said through gritted teeth.

'Leave what?' Nick frowned, gesturing for her to wait as he said goodbye to the physiotherapist. 'Thanks for that, Amber, it's been very helpful.'

'Any time, Nick. Call me if you need to discuss Rory's ambulation programme further.' Amber smiled and Eden felt her already gritted teeth starting to grind as the tall slender physio continued talking, completely unfazed by Eden's presence. 'In fact, call me anyway— I'll look forward to it.'

'Well, she certainly knows how to get her message across!' Eden bristled as Amber waltzed off, her back impossibly straight, flicking her blonde hair as she did so.

'She was just being friendly.' Nick laughed. 'Just what is it that you have against physios?'

'Their glowing health,' Eden moaned. 'Their toned bodies and white smiles. I could go on for ever. I haven't yet met one with a single vice. You just know that they'll be tucking into a cottage cheese salad for lunch, know for a fact that they don't smoke.'

'Neither do you,' Nick pointed out, and then shook his head. 'Let's not change the subject. This is my ward, Eden, and if there's a problem I need to know about it.'

'There isn't a problem,' Eden insisted. 'At least, not any more.'

'Eden, you've lost me.'

Taking a deep breath, she finally faced him. 'Donna just called an impromptu meeting to discuss the revised Christmas roster.'

'Oh.'

Instantly his eyes glazed over. The nursing roster was way down on Nick Watson's list of priorities. So long as his precious patients were happy then so was he. But, Eden reminded herself, Nick was the one who'd stopped her, who had demanded that she tell him what was wrong, and Nick who had insisted that she voice her problem. And voice it she would.

Loudly!

'This will be my second Christmas on this

ward,' Eden choked. 'And now it seems I'll have to work night shifts for both! Donna's been hounding me to use up my annual leave as I've got five weeks owing. I was supposed to be having a full week off, given that last year….' The spitfire that was raging was doused a touch as Eden realised the inappropriateness of this conversation, but Nick, with a very noticeable edge to his voice, quickly filled her in.

'You had to work over the Christmas and New Year period because of what happened to Teaghan…'

Damn! She didn't say it, but the word spat like a hot chip between them. Eden slammed her forehead with her hand, wishing she could take it all back, wishing that Nick hadn't chosen that particular moment to come out of his office and demand to know what the problem was.

Eden had been so angry she'd chosen to take her fifteen-minute coffee-break away from the ward in an attempt to cool down before she said something she'd surely regret, but unfortunately she had done just that. The tragic events that had taken place the previous December hadn't just affected Eden's off-duty roster—the whole ward had gone into numb shock when Teaghan Camm, Associate Charge Nurse and fiancée to Nick Watson, had driven home after a night shift and apparently fallen asleep at the wheel. She'd suffered injuries so severe that she hadn't even made it into the emergency resuscitation room.

Eden could still recall that morning as if it had happened only yesterday.

As the nurse in charge that morning, it had been she, Eden, who had taken the call from Emergency. She had heard how the vibrant young woman, who had left the ward only an hour or so before now lay dead a few floors below. It had been Eden who had located Teaghan's personal file and relayed her parents' telephone number to Sharon, the nurse supervisor who had been with Teaghan in Emergency. She could still hear Sharon's devastated voice as she'd asked Eden whether she wanted her to come up and tell the staff.

'I'll do it,' Eden had said, not wanting to but knowing Sharon should be there to wait for Teaghan's parents to arrive.

'What about…?' Sharon had hesitated and Eden had been too stunned, too shocked to fill in the gap, just screwed her eyes closed as Sharon had stumbled on. 'Nick has to hear this privately, Eden.'

'I'll tell him first, away from everyone else.'

'Perhaps I should send up Brad, the emergency consultant,' Sharon suggested. 'Maybe another doctor should be the one to tell him—although whoever it is who breaks the news, it's not going to change the outcome.'

Looking out of her office, Eden had seen one of the porters stopping to talk to the ward domestic, her shocked expression telling Eden that the unpalatable news had already started filtering its way through. She had seen Nick at a patient's bedside, sharing a joke with the child's mother, utterly oblivious to the fact that in the same building at that very moment, his young fiancée had lain dead.

'I think I'd better tell him now.' Eden swallowed hard. 'The news just hit the ward. I don't want him to hear this on the floor. Send Brad up, though. I'm sure Nick will have a lot of questions.'

It was among the hardest things she had ever done in her life. As a senior nurse on a busy paediatric ward, Eden had seen more than her fair share of tragedy, had sat more times than she wanted to remember with devastated parents as terrible news had been broken, had even delivered it herself when the occasion had merited it, but to survive she managed to retain some degree of professional detachment. Though tears were sometimes shed, they were always controlled. She constantly reminded herself that, as much as she was hurting, it was worse, far, far worse for the parents, and the last thing they needed was an overly emotional nurse.

But this was personal.

Very personal.

She hadn't particularly liked Teaghan, had never taken to the rather loud, over-confident woman, but she'd never in a million years have wished this on her, and Eden was realistic enough to realise that her own judgement of the woman was probably tainted. Tainted by the fact that she, along with every other woman at the Royal, was just a tiny bit in love with Nick Watson.

'Nick.' He looked up as she came out of the office, gave a tiny questioning frown as she'd asked him if she could have a word.

'What's the problem?' Blond, happy, smiling and utterly oblivious, he strode in, took a seat when she asked him to do so. 'What have I done wrong this time?' He grinned.

'Nothing,' Eden croaked, then cleared her throat, willing herself to get on with it.

They were friends.

Sure, she'd only been there three months, but since the first shift they'd worked together they'd clicked, gently teasing each other, pre-empting each other's jokes, moaning together as friends did.

And now she had to break his heart.

'Nick, there was an accident in the city this morning…'

'Yeah,' Nick moaned, 'that's why I was late. Why?' His voice was suddenly serious. 'Are there kids involved? Should I go down to Emergency?'

'Nick.' She halted him almost harshly, and as his green eyes met hers they widened just a fraction, perhaps realising that this had nothing to do with work and everything to do with him. She felt as if she were wielding an axe, watching him wince as each blow was delivered. 'It was Teaghan's car.'

'No.' He shook his head, absolutely denying it, but a muscle was pounding in his cheek, his jaw muscles tensing as he refuted her words. 'She wasn't going anywhere near the city. She'd just done a night shift. Teaghan's at home, asleep…'

'Nick, it *was* Teaghan in the car,' Eden said firmly. 'She was wearing her ID badge, and Sharon Kennedy, the nurse supervisor, has confirmed that it's her. She was brought here a short while ago…' She knew, because of her training, that there must be no room for doubt as you delivered the news, that words like 'she didn't suffer' or 'everything possible was done' had no place yet in this horrible conversation. They had to come later. There could be no room for false hope. Raising her mental axe, trembling inside as she did so, Eden delivered the final, appalling blow. 'Nick, Teaghan was pronounced dead on arrival.'

And she watched—watched as her words felled him. Watched that carefree face crumple before her eyes, watched as he seemed to age a decade in a matter of seconds. Every sound was somehow magnified—a scream from a child on the ward, a baby crying in the background, IV pumps singing loudly for attention, the linen trolley clattering past her office, the world moving on as it stopped in its tracks for Nick. She didn't know what to do, knew there was nothing she could say that could make it even a tiny bit better. She crossed the short distance between them and put her arms around his tense shoulders, felt the squeeze of his hand as he gripped her arm, the shudder of his breath as he leant his head on her chest, one low sob the only noise he made. His pain was palpable and she held him, held him for a time so small it was barely there, caught him as he went into freefall, tears spilling out of her eyes as she witnessed his agony.

'I have to go to her…'

The tiny moment to process was over, replaced now with a blinding need to see Teaghan, to maybe put right a million wrongs, to do something, anything. He stood up, dragging a hand over his mouth, swallowing back the scream he was surely suppressing. His eyes again met hers, tortured eyes that begged for answers, begged her to take it all back, to somehow erase what she'd said. But all she could do was stare back helplessly, tears spilling down her cheeks as she felt his devastation. Then he was gone. His arm knocked a pile of papers off her desk in his haste to get to his fiancée, the chair toppled over as he dashed past it, he collided with the porter who was wheeling the linen trolley. His feet pounded as he ran down the corridor and Eden just stood there, white-faced and shaking, not moving until Brad Jenkins, the emergency consultant, appeared grim-faced at the door, taking in the chaos Nick had left in his wake.

'You just missed him,' Eden said, the words shivering out of her chattering lips. She braced herself to call the staff in, to tell the rest of her colleagues the terrible news. 'He's gone to be with Teaghan.'

'I'm sorry.' Eden hadn't said it on that fateful day, but she said it now, turning troubled eyes to him. Here she was moaning about the roster, and the fact that she'd had to work last year as well. It suddenly seemed beyond petty, given all Nick had been through, given what had happened to Teaghan. 'That was absolutely thoughtless of me,' Eden apologised again, and Nick gave a small forgiving smile.

'So why do you have to work this year?'

'It doesn't matter.' Horribly embarrassed, cringing inside, Eden made to go, but again Nick halted her.

'Let's talk in here,' he suggested, gesturing for her to go into his office, but Eden shook her head.

'The nursing roster isn't your problem, Nick. I was just letting off a bit of steam.'

'Then let it off over a decent cup of coffee.'

He walked back into his office, clearly expecting Eden to follow, and for a moment she stood there, not quite sure she was up to an impromptu chat with Nick right now. Since Donna had dropped her bomb about the Christmas roster, Eden's emotions had been bubbling dangerously close to the surface, and fifteen minutes alone with Nick was the *last* thing that was going to calm her down.

Nick was the main reason she had wanted Christmas off in the first place!

A week at home with her family, a week away from the city, a week of horse riding and clearing her mind, far away from the pressure cooker she found herself in whenever Nick was near.

'Eden!' Nick's impatient voice snapped her attention back. She took a deep breath and headed into his office, determined not to let him glimpse the effect he had on her.

Nick Watson's ego was already big enough, without another boost.

'Still take sugar?' Nick asked, not looking up.

'Please.' Perching herself on a chair, Eden forced a smile as Nick handed her a coffee, pleased that her hands were steady as she took the cup. 'I really am sorry about what I said…'

'Don't worry.' Nick waved a hand as he sat down. 'I'm OK.'

'You're sure?' Eden checked, but she wasn't just talking about her little *faux pas* earlier. 'This time of year must be awful for you.'

'Actually, no.' Nick shook his head. 'I'm too busy to even start feeling sorry for myself. There's too many parties and dinners and, of course—'

'Women,' Eden finished for him with a slight edge to her voice, which she quickly fought to check.

'I was about to say work.' Nick grinned. 'But now you mention it…! Anyway, enough about my social life. How come they're making you work over Christmas again? I thought the ward policy was one year on, one year off.'

'It was,' Eden sighed, 'until Ruth went off on early maternity leave. *Apparently* her blood pressure's high.'

'Apparently?' Nick raised an eyebrow, picking up the tiny note of cynicism and Eden winced.

'That sounded so bitchy, didn't it? But I've guessed for months that she wasn't going to make it to Christmas, especially given the fact that she was down to work night shifts on Christmas Eve and Boxing Day. Donna called us all into the office earlier and asked for volunteers to take Ruth's shifts.'

'I'm assuming you didn't put your hand up.'

'No!' Eden took a sip of her coffee before she continued, 'No one did. And then it started.'

'What started?'

'"Timmy's only two" or "It's Jamie's first Christmas". Even Becky, who's supposed to be my friend, chimed in that it's "Conner's last Christmas while he still believes in Santa".' Nick grinned as she mimicked her various colleagues' voices and a tiny smile wobbled on Eden's lips. 'I don't have a defence, given that I'm a paediatric nurse on a paediatric ward, I, of all people, should understand that children want their mums to be there on Christmas morning so Donna asked if I'd mind working it.'

'You could have said no,' Nick pointed out, and then laughed. 'Hell, Eden, why didn't you just say that you weren't prepared to do it? Why can't you just say no to Donna?'

'I tried!' Eden wailed.

'How?'

'I pointed out that if I work a night shift on Christmas Eve I can hardly be expected to drive to Coffs Harbour on Christmas morning unless they want me to doze off at the...' Her voice trailed off again as the conversation tipped where it shouldn't. 'Last year my dad drove all the way down to Sydney and stayed at my flat overnight just so that I could be with my family on Christmas Day, but it was just too much for him. It's a six-hour drive after all—it was actually too much for me as well. We both ended up sound asleep for the best part of the day—just about missed Christmas altogether. I can't ask him to do it again this year.'

'What about your flatmate, Jim?' he asked. 'What's he doing for Christmas?'

'He's going to Queensland for the Christmas break. Actually, he's been trying to persuade me to come with him and his friend. Maybe I should tell Donna that I'm going to be away and take him up on it. '

'Maybe you should.'

Eden pulled a face. 'I don't think so. There's only so much damage one's liver can take. As much beer and barbequed prawns as you can stomach isn't really my idea of Christmas.'

'You can't be on your own.' Nick shook his head, but Eden just gave a wry smile.

'Believe me, Nick, I'd rather be. I've already had about three invites for Christmas dinner from my guilty colleagues…'

'And?'

'Timmy may only be two…' Eden rolled her eyes '…but he's an absolute monster. And as much as I adore Conner, I see enough kids' tantrums in a day's work…' She gave a small shrug. 'You get the picture!'

'I do.' Nick grinned back. And it was funny, Eden mused, that even after a year of relative silence they could slip back so easily into their own shorthand, pick up on the tiny vibes without explanation. 'And I suppose the fact that Becky's also a strict vegan had nothing to do with it.'

'Caught.' Eden managed a weak smile. 'I guess if I want my turkey and ham, I'll have to cook it myself.'

'There's always the canteen.'

The look Eden shot him wasn't particularly friendly but Nick merely roared with laughter. 'It will probably be in the high thirties,' Nick pointed out. 'The last thing you'll want is a huge roast.'

'Wrong.' Eden pouted. 'I love Christmas dinner, pudding, mince pies…' She closed her eyes for an indulgent second, imagining her parents' dining room at home, the air-conditioning on full blast as the table groaned under the weight of ham and turkey, roast pork, little sausages wrapped in bacon and mountains of Christmas crackers with their cheesy presents and even cheesier jokes. But Nick threw a bucket of water over her fantasy.

'Well, if it makes you feel any better, I'd love to have your problem. I've practically begged to work this Christmas but the powers that be have decided, given my *circumstances,* that they know best, and that what I really need is a nice little break over the festive season with my family.' Nick's low groan told Eden that it was the last place he wanted to be, and she blinked at him in bewilderment.

'But it's Christmas!' she said, and it should have been explanation enough, but as Nick just grimaced, Eden let out a wail of indignation. 'It's Christmas,' she said again. 'How could you not want to spend it with them? I thought you adored your family?'

'I do.' Nick rolled his eyes. 'And they adore me, so much so that they want to see me happy, which I am, of course, but they beg to differ. Happy to them means…'

'You *can* say it, Nick.' Eden smiled.

'OK.' He took a deep theatrical breath. 'They want to see me in a relationship!'

'I thought you were.' Eden blinked innocently. 'With Shelly from Emergency—oh, no, sorry, I meant Phoebe from ICU.' Another blink, a tiny frown as she tried to place a name, and she heard Nick's intake of breath as he realised she was teasing him. 'What about that intern—oh, what is her name…?' She clicked her fingers a couple of times as Nick actually managed a small blush. 'Tanya, that's the one. Whatever happened to her?'

She already knew the answer! Nick's initial devastation at Teaghan's death had slowly been replaced by a curious arrogance as he'd headed off the rails, his undeniable charm working its way around the hospital and leaving devastation in its wake. But even though it was considered almost an insult not to have been dated by Nick during the last twelve months, not once had Nick attempted to cross the line with Eden. And even though she valued what was left of his friendship, even though the last thing she wanted was to be another of his conquests,

Nick's indifference to her on the romantic front was breaking Eden's heart.

'Tanya and I are just friends,' Nick said. 'You're reading far too much into it."

'*We're* just friends, Nick.' Draining her coffee-cup, trying not to show just how much that admission hurt, Eden stood up. 'Or we used to be.'

'What's that supposed to mean?' Nick asked, but Eden just shrugged.

'Nothing.'

'It didn't sound like nothing. What did you mean?'

'Just that things have changed lately,' Eden admitted. 'Sometimes I feel as if I hardly know you any more.'

'You're being daft.' Nick grinned.

'Perhaps I am, but take it from me, what Tanya feels isn't merely friendly, so tread carefully. Anyway, enough already about your love life, Nick. I'd better get back out there. I can hear the meal trolley coming and I've a feeling someone's about to kick up a fuss when they find out I swapped her order.'

'Priscilla?' Nick checked almost needlessly, referring to a nine-year-old with a penchant for chicken nuggets. 'I'm going to have to speak to her mother again.'

'Well, tread carefully,' Eden warned. 'Remember that she's a high-profile lawyer.'

'So maybe she'll appreciate some straight talking,' Nick countered. 'Hell, we're so bogged down in politically correct jargon these days, so terrified of being sued, it's a wonder anything useful gets done in this place; Priscilla's a great kid, but unless someone spells it out to Rose, unless someone actually sits that woman down and tells her to stop feeding her kid rubbish, we may as well send her daughter home with a packet of cholesterol-lowering pills and a post-dated referral to a psychologist to deal with the *issues* of bullying.'

Eden shot him a worried look but, as politically incorrect as Nick could be at times, more often than not his straight talking hit the nail on the head.

'The other kids are starting to tease her.'

'If I were nine, I'd tease her,' Nick moaned, and thankfully he wasn't looking so he didn't see a tiny smile flash on her lips as she pictured Nick Watson as a cheeky blond nine-year-old. 'What the hell is Rose doing, calling her Princess in front of the other kids?'

'It's her pet name.'

'Then she should save it for home. Are you going to do it ?' Nick added as she headed for the door. 'Work Christmas, I mean?'

'It looks that way,' Eden sighed.

'You need a baby of your own,' Nick said with another grin, and Eden gave a wry smile back.

'It's probably the only way I can guarantee getting next Christmas off—I'd better step on it.'

'You'd better,' Nick responded dryly. 'Given that they take nine months…'

'I was referring to work, Nick,' Eden said.

CHAPTER TWO

PRISCILLA, or Princess as her mother called her, was in for investigation into her recurrent constipation and abdominal pain, which had culminated in many trips to her local GP and a lot of absences from school. As a private patient, initially her mother had demanded a single room for her daughter, but thankfully Nick had been able to persuade Rose that her daughter would benefit from being among her peers, and after a rather prolonged negotiation Rose had finally agreed.

Even though she was in a public ward, Priscilla still demanded private patient attention, pressing the call bell incessantly, complaining loudly about the food and the lack of her own television—to the amusement of her fellow patients, who were starting to tease the little girl and calling her by her nickname of Princess, though not in the affectionate way her mother delivered it.

As annoying as Priscilla could be, as demanding as she was, despite the other nurses' grumbles when allocated to look after her, Eden actually enjoyed looking after the spoilt little girl. Fiercely intelligent, she had a wry sense of humour. Very pretty, she was also very overweight and had her exhausted working single mother wrapped around her rather podgy little fingers. She was completely used to getting her own way—and quickly, please! Since she'd discovered that the call bell by her bed summoned attention quickly, Priscilla was abusing it to the max, despite the fact she wasn't on bed rest. However, before Eden again explained that fact, first she had to be sure that there was nothing wrong with the little girl.

'What's the problem, Priscilla?' Eden asked, smiling as she made her way over to the bed.

'This isn't the dinner I ordered.' Frowning down at her plate, Priscilla stabbed at a defenceless piece of roast chicken and vegetables. 'Mummy ticked the chicken nuggets for me—look.' She held out the menu card for Eden, but Eden didn't need to read it to know what was on it.

'You had nuggets for dinner last night,' Eden explained patiently, 'and the previous night as well.'

'Because I like nuggets.'

'Do you remember that Dr Nick said you were to have more variety in your diet? Well, instead of having chicken nuggets, why not try having some roast chicken and some of the lovely vegetables?'

'I don't like vegetables.' Priscilla pouted, her bottom lip wobbling, tears filling her big blue eyes, and Eden was grateful that Priscilla's mother wasn't there because it was at about this point that Priscilla was used to adults giving in. But Eden stood her ground, undoing the little pack of fruit juice and pouring some out for Priscilla.

'When Mummy comes I'll tell her to go and get me some nuggets from the take-away.'

'You're going to turn into a nugget one of these days.' Nick was there, ruffling Priscilla's hair, grinning broadly and completely ignoring her tears. 'I told Eden that you were going to eat some veggies for me tonight, Priscilla. Now, you're not going to make me look silly, are you?'

'I hate veggies,' Priscilla snarled, slamming down her knife and fork with a clatter that alerted her fellow patients to the start of yet another of Priscilla's rather too frequent dramas.

'Come on Princess, eat your veggies,' Rory, a cheeky ten-year-old with his leg in traction, called out.

'Yeah, come on, Princess,' Declan, a five-year-old post-tonsillectomy patient chimed in.

'Cut it out, guys,' Eden warned, pulling the curtains and shutting out the delighted audience while Nick stood firm with his patient.

'Roast chicken and vegetables are what's for dinner tonight—' He didn't finish. Priscilla's meal tray crashing loudly to the floor, courtesy of a flash of temper, interrupted the conversation. Her angry face stared defiantly at both

Eden and Nick, awaiting their reaction as a few cheers erupted from the other side of the curtains.

'Whoops,' Nick said calmly, which clearly wasn't the reaction Priscilla had been expecting. Her angry face puckered into a frown, her expression changing from fury to utter indignation as Nick calmly continued talking. 'Not to worry. Accidents happen. Eden can ring down to the canteen and order you another dinner.'

The tears started again, angry furious tears, her pretty face purple with rage.

'Do you need a hand?' Becky asked, arriving with the mop and bucket as Eden picked the remains of the meal off the floor. 'Her mother has just arrived,' she added in a low tone to Nick as she bent down to help Eden.

'What's going on?' Rose Tarrington clipped into the ward on smart high heels, her petite frame in an expensive chocolate brown suit, well made-up eyes frowning as she pulled open the curtains and surveyed the mess.

'Priscilla knocked over her dinner,' Nick responded calmly. 'Sister's just going to order her another one.'

'But she won't eat that.' Rose pointed a manicured finger at the messy remains. 'I know you want her to have some variety, but you can hardly expect her to suddenly start eating roast meat and vegetables overnight!'

'The other children are,' Nick broke in, staring around the ward at the other three children, all eating their dinners.

'Look, Princess.' Rose made her way over to her daughter's bedside and cuddled the distraught child. 'Why don't you do as the doctor and nurses say? Eat your dinner and then, if you do, I'll go over the road and get you some ice cream.'

'Could I have a word at the nurses' station, please, Ms Tarrington?' Nick broke in, and Eden watched as the woman stiffened.

'I'm just talking to my daughter.'

'It won't take long.' Nick's voice was even but it had a certain ring to it that told everyone present he wasn't about to take no for an answer.

'Becky can stay with Priscilla,' Nick instructed. 'Eden, would you mind joining us, please?'

Eden rather wished he'd allocated her to clean up the mess and sort out Priscilla. A nine-year-old throwing a tantrum she could deal with blindfolded, but a brutal dose of honesty, as only Nick could deliver it, wasn't going to be particularly pleasant, though it was called for.

The endless talks with the nursing staff, doctors and dieticians clearly hadn't made the slightest bit of difference to Rose or Priscilla's behaviour and now, Eden guessed as she followed Nick to the nurses' station, the kid gloves were off. Nick's only priority was his patients.

'Have a seat.' Nick gestured to the tense woman, barely waiting till she was seated before diving in.

'I've asked Sister Hadley to sit in so that we can all be on the same page,' Nick explained. 'For Priscilla's sake, we all need to be taking the same approach.

'We don't seem to be getting very far, do we, Rose?' Nick started softly, but Rose Tarrington clearly wasn't in any mood for a gentle lead-in. Brittle and defensive, she stared angrily back at Nick.

'Perhaps if you stopped focussing on my daughter's diet and found out just what the hell the problem is with her stomach, we'd start to make some progress. Priscilla's been in here a week now and apart from a few blood tests and an X-ray, she's had nothing done for her.' Rose's hands clenched in frustration, her legs tightly crossed. She was the complete opposite to Nick, who sat relaxed and open in the chair opposite. 'Oh, and an ultrasound,' Rose spat, more as an afterthought. 'We could have done all that as outpatients. I'm not asking for favours, but given the fact my daughter's a private patient…'

'That has no bearing.' Nick shook his head. 'I have a mixture of private and public patients on my list, Rose, and I can assure you they all receive the same treatment from both me and the staff on the ward. Yes, as a private patient Priscilla could, no doubt, have had all these investigations done speedily as an outpatient, but, as I explained to you in Emergency when I admitted your daughter, given that Priscilla has already missed out on a third of her schooling this year, it really is imperative that we find out what's causing her abdominal pain and causing her to miss so much school. Which…' As Rose opened her mouth to argue, Nick shook his head, speaking over the angry woman. 'Which we have,' he said firmly. 'The abdominal X-ray showed that Priscilla was chronically constipated, the ultrasound told me that there was nothing acutely wrong and her blood work confirmed my clinical diagnosis. Priscilla is anaemic, her cholesterol is high…' He paused for a second, only this time Rose didn't jump in to argue, this time Rose closed her eyes as Nick gently but firmly continued. 'Now, I could put on her on some iron tablets. However, that would only cause further constipation. To counter that, I could prescribe a fibre supplement, but I don't think Priscilla would drink it. I could, of course, give her laxatives, but the thing is I'm not prepared to do that when all she needs is a varied, healthy diet and an increase in her physical activity.'

'That's all she needs, is it?' Rose's tired, angry eyes were bulging as she spoke. 'You've seen what she's like when she doesn't get her own way. I work ten-hour days and, yes, it's easier to pick up a take-away than to start cooking, but what am I supposed to do when it's the only thing she'll eat. I can hardly let her go to bed without eating…'

'You could,' Nick replied, but Rose just scoffed.

'You obviously don't have children, Doctor. Don't you think I already feel guilty enough about the hours I work, without spending every evening fighting with my daughter over what she wants for dinner and sending her to bed hungry? No doubt you'll be telling me soon to cut down my hours and start spending more *quality* time…' Tears came then, choking, angry tears, her tiny, exhausted frame heaving, her hand pressing on her mouth as she tried to hold it all in. Nick still calmly sat there, not remotely embarrassed, pulling a couple of tissues from the box on the desk and handing them to her before pressing on.

'I wouldn't dream of telling you to cut down your hours, Rose. I'm aware that you're a single parent. You're doing an amazing job—'

'Don't patronise me,' Rose snarled as she blew her nose. 'Don't try and tell me I'm doing well when you clearly think I'm an unfit mother.'

'No one thinks that.' Eden said, her voice a gentle interlude from the painful conversation. 'We're not ganging up on you, Rose, we all just want to do the best we can for Priscilla. Nick isn't suggesting that you're an unfit parent. If that were the case, we'd be having this conversation in an office with a case worker present so, please, let's try and not go there.'

Standing, Eden fetched a drink of water for Rose from the cooler, a tiny nod the only response from Rose as she handed it to her. Nick waited as Rose had a drink and then continued.

'Eden's right. I don't think that for a moment.' Nick shook his head. 'And you're right as well. I don't have kids, but my sister is a busy

GP with three little ones and is in the process of getting a divorce. I've heard from Lily all about the guilt, the endless juggling and the pressures of trying to do the right thing.'

'It's just so hard,' Rose choked.

'If it carries on like this, Rose, it's going to get harder,' Nick said as Rose frowned. 'Priscilla is so constipated that if the situation continues, very soon she could end up with some overflow.' When Rose frowned, Nick clarified his words and Rose closed her eyes as he did so. 'She could have episodes of faecal incontinence. Priscilla has already told some of the nursing staff that she gets teased at school about her weight. Can you imagine how much harder it will be for her if she starts to soil her pants as well?'

Eden half expected an argument, but all the fight seemed to go out of Rose. The hotshot lawyer was gone, leaving just a terrified mum sitting on the chair. 'She already has,' Rose whispered through pale, trembling lips. 'Only once, but…it's all my fault, isn't it?'

'We're not going there, remember? We're

here to deal with the things we can change, and the past isn't one of them.' Nick gave a very nice smile, peeling another wad of tissues out of the box. 'Come on, Rose, blow your nose and stop the tears and let's work out what we're going to do.' He glanced over at Eden and she took her cue.

'At the moment Priscilla's used to getting food as a reward and she's using it to her advantage,' Eden explained. 'For example, you said to her tonight that if she ate her dinner then you'd get her an ice cream.'

'It's all I could think of to get her to eat her dinner,' Rose admitted.

'How about, leaving out the "if",' Eden suggested. 'Try "Eat your dinner, Priscilla, and then I'll read to you" or "then we'll watch a movie together" or "then I'll help you with your homework".'

'Spend some *quality* time with her?' Rose asked, only this time it was said without contempt.

'For want of a word, only in this case it's time you would usually spend arguing,' Eden responded. 'In the morning, you can do the same: "Eat your breakfast and then you can watch some television."'

'Make it non-negotiable,' Nick said, 'but at the same time make out it's no big deal. Be matter-of-fact about it—she *has* to eat her meals, and by that I mean the meals you provide for her, not the ones she demands.

'And I choose my words carefully, Rose,' Nick winked, and to Eden's amazement Rose actually managed a pale smile as he continued. 'I'm not telling you to grow a vegetable patch and start steaming broccoli every night. Just a normal balanced diet is all Priscilla needs— you, too, no doubt. I'm assuming here that you're not tucking into the fries and nuggets yourself?'

Rose shook her head.

'Cheese on toast around midnight?' Nick asked.

'Something like that,' Rose admitted.

'Me, too,' Nick sighed. 'How about you, Eden?'

'I'm more a bowl-of-cereal girl.'

'Stop boasting.' Nick grinned. 'We're all guilty of it, Rose. We've all got jobs that demand too much of us so we grab something to eat when we can or when we absolutely have to. But as you pointed out, Eden and I don't have kids, so we *can* mess up our own health. Look, if you can afford it, why not get your meals delivered for a few weeks? You could choose your menus together, there are a few companies that provide that type of service.'

'And that would be OK?'

'Absolutely.' Nick nodded.

'And,' Eden added, 'if it makes things easier for you, for the next couple of days why not let us deal with Priscilla at mealtimes?'

'Shouldn't *I* be telling her?' Rose asked wisely. 'Given that I'm the one that's going to be dealing with her at home.'

'You should,' Eden said, 'but it's going to be difficult the first few times. Priscilla isn't going to take very kindly to the rules suddenly changing and we can take some of the strain for you, so long as you support us. As Nick said, if we're all working as a team there's a better chance of getting results. Why don't you come in at meal-times and if Priscilla starts to kick up, tell her that you're going to the canteen for a coffee and that the nurses will ring down once she's finished her dinner?'

'You'd do that?'

'Definitely.' Eden nodded, peering over Rose's shoulder as an orderly arrived with a fresh meal. 'How about we start now?'

'She's not going to like it,' Rose warned.

'Good,' Nick said, standing up and shaking Rose's hand warmly. 'Because I'm sure you could use a coffee and a bit of time alone to think about what we've just said. And for the record, Rose, I wasn't being patronising before. You are doing an amazing job—Priscilla's funny, intelligent and incredibly perceptive.'

'Thank you.' Rose blushed. 'She really is my little princess.' Nick opened his mouth, then clearly thought better of it. Now, perhaps, was not the time to tell Rose to curb her pet name, at least around Priscilla's peers. 'I'll just go to the washroom and freshen up. I don't want her to see that I've been crying.'

As Rose scurried off, Eden expected Nick to do the same, but instead he remained. 'Thanks for your help. Hopefully some of it got through to Rose.'

'I think a lot of it got through,' Eden replied generously. 'You were really good with her.'

'Probably because I've had a lot of practice around tearful women lately,' Nick said, but as Eden's lips pursed his face broke into a slightly incredulous smile. 'You're really quick to think the worst of me, aren't you, Eden? When I said I'd been around tearful women lately, I was actually referring to my sister, Lily.'

'Oh.' Blushing, Eden scuffed the floor with her foot. 'Well, you can hardly blame me for assuming…' Her voice trailed off, and Nick did absolutely nothing to fill the uncomfortable silence. Eden willed Rose to hurry back, terrified that if she looked up, Nick might catch a glimpse of the jealous feelings that seemed to choke her whenever she pictured him with another woman. However, her mouth was moving ahead of her mind and wretched emotions were taking over. Wincing inside, yet completely unable to stop herself, a tiny slice of truth came out. 'I just don't like seeing people used, that's all.'

'Used?' She could hear the frown in his voice without looking up, and Eden knew she'd gone too far, knew that she had to pull back now before irretrievable damage was done, before Nick realised how much she was hurting. Forcing a very cheeky smile, she dragged her eyes back to his.

'Yes, used, Nick. Just because you're blond and gorgeous, it doesn't mean that you don't have feelings, too!' And even though he smiled at her joke, it didn't quite reach his eyes and Eden knew her attempt at recovery hadn't quite succeeded. 'I'm allowed to worry about you— that's what friends do.'

The smile was back in his eyes now, and Eden gave an inward sigh of relief as Rose appeared.

'Good luck,' Nick called as Eden and Rose headed back towards Priscilla's bedside, just in time to see Becky setting up the replacement meal tray.

'Oh, look.' Rose smiled. 'Roast chicken—

yum!' Her tone was a touch forced, but Eden was pleased to see how hard she was trying. 'Now, come on, eat up your dinner and then you can read to me.'

'I'm not eating that filth!' Priscilla snarled. Her hand moved towards the tray, but Eden was too quick for her.

'Oh, no.' Eden held onto the tray, holding the young girl's angry glare. 'There are plenty more trays down in the canteen, Priscilla. I can ring down for more all evening if I have to, but we're not wasting good food like that.'

'Well, I'm not eating it.' Priscilla's bottom lip was working overtime and she squeezed out a tear for effect. 'Mummy, I don't like roast chicken!'

'That's what's for dinner tonight, Priscilla.' Rose took a deep breath and Eden felt sorry for her, knowing how hard it must be for her to be firm when her daughter lay in a hospital bed. 'Now, it looks so nice that I'm going down to the canteen to have some dinner myself. When you're finished, Eden here will ring me and I'll come back up.'

'Mummy!' Priscilla wasn't squeezing tears out now—they were coming thick and fast of their own accord. 'Mummy, don't leave me!'

'As soon as your dinner's finished, darling, I'll come back up.' Hiding tears of her own, Rose turned quickly, hurrying out of the ward. Eden ran after her as Becky stayed with a shrieking Priscilla.

'She'll be fine,' Eden soothed. 'You did so well.'

'I can't do this every night,' Rose sobbed.

'You won't have to,' Eden said. 'As soon as Priscilla realises that you're serious, she'll start eating properly. Rose, just remember that all you are asking is for her to eat her dinner, not walk on hot coals. There's nothing unreasonable or unfair about what you're doing.'

'I know,' Rose gulped.

'Now, go and have a coffee or dinner. I promise that we'll look after her and as soon as she's made a reasonable effort with her dinner, I'll ring you.'

'And if she doesn't?'

'I'll ring down for you anyway.' Eden smiled. 'But let's stay positive.'

In fact, by the time Eden returned to the bedside, the tears had stopped and Priscilla was sitting upright with her arms folded pointedly, not looking up as Eden made her way over.

'Thanks, Becky.'

'No worries.' Becky grinned, scooting off to check on her own patients.

'Your mum has just gone to have some dinner,' Eden said, picking up a rather impressive book on Priscilla's bedside. 'Is this yours?'

When Priscilla didn't answer, Eden pressed on, unperturbed. 'It's a huge book for a nine-year-old.'

'It's easy.' Priscilla bristled.

'Well, I don't think so—all those funny names and spells and trying to work out who the baddy is….'

'You've read it?' Priscilla blinked, curiosity overriding her anger for a moment.

'Not this one,' Eden admitted, 'but I've read

four in the series and I'm hoping someone will get me this one for Christmas.'

'But it's a kid's book.'

'So?' Sitting down at the bedside, Eden peeled off the cover on Priscilla's dinner. 'Come on, Priscilla, eat your dinner and then I'll call downstairs for Mum to come up. She said you were going to read to her tonight, and she's really looking forward to it.' Pretending to ignore her, Eden concentrated on the blurb at the back of the book as Eden slowly picked up her knife and fork.

'I don't like broccoli.'

Eden flicked the pages, deliberately not looking up.

'Eden, I *really* don't like broccoli.'

'Neither do I.' Eden smiled. 'OK. How about you eat everything else? If you do that, you can leave the broccoli.'

'I don't like carrots.'

'Priscilla.' Eden's voice held a warning. 'If you eat all your carrots, potato and chicken, *then* you can leave the broccoli.' Turning back to the book, she flicked the pages. 'Where are you up to?'

To an onlooker, Eden knew she probably looked as if she was doing nothing but sitting on the bed as Priscilla slowly worked her way through her meal, but, Eden knew exactly what she was doing; knew she had the best job in the world. Rose had trusted her enough to go down to the canteen and Priscilla was actually eating her dinner. They might not be cutting-edge science, but tonight she and Nick had hopefully made a difference, a huge difference, in a little girl's life.

And Priscilla did very well!

Eden's heart swelled with pride as finally the plate was if not clean then almost so. Priscilla had even had a small piece of the broccoli.

'Well done, honey.' Eden grinned and picked up the tray, careful not too make too much of a fuss but also wanting to acknowledge Priscilla's effort. 'How about I go and ring down to the canteen for your mum?'

'Are you on in the morning?' Priscilla asked, and Eden shook her head.

'I'm on another late shift. I'll come and check on you a bit later. You enjoy reading to your mum.'

'How did Priscilla get on with her dinner?' Nick asked a while later, when Becky was on her supper break and Eden was giving a grumpy six-month-old named Justin the last of his bottle.

Eden loved this time of night on the children's ward. At seven the main lights were switched off and the curtains drawn and, despite the light Sydney evening outside, the whole ward was plunged into darkness, filled with the sounds of babies' and toddlers' final protests as their parents or nurses soothed them off to sleep, the background drone of the television in the older children's rooms. Usually with Donna, the unit manager, gone and most doctors long since headed for home there was a chance for Eden to take her time feeding a baby or sit on a bed and have a chat with a lonely patient or just catch up with the mountain of paperwork involved in nursing these days. It was one of the main reasons she often volunteered for the late shift.

'Good.' Eden said. 'Rose is going to go through tomorrow's menu with her a bit later on and I'll pass it all on to the night staff. Hopefully, if we all keep it up, she'll be a different girl in a few days. Becky and I are both on another late shift tomorrow, which will make things easier when Rose comes in. How come you're still here?' she added.

'I'm not.' Picking up his briefcase, he gave a tired smile. 'Unless my pager goes off between now and the car park. I'll see you tomorrow.'

'See, you, Nick.' Eden smiled back. 'Have a good night.'

'I will if you don't call!'

No doubt a thousand doctors were jokingly saying those exact words to a thousand nurses even as Nick spoke them, but for Eden they hurt like hell.

The hardest part of the entire day was about to ensue.

She kept a professional smile in place as he picked up his briefcase and walked out of the ward, wondering who he was on his way to see, wondering who was filling the long hours till she saw him again.

Wondering where the loyal man who had been engaged to Teaghan had disappeared to…

Maybe he felt her eyes on him, but for some reason as he reached the door he turned around, then walked back the length of the ward in long purposeful strides. Eden figured he must have forgotten to sign for something or was going to remind her about a patient.

'I've been thinking about our mutual problem.'

'Mutual problem?' Eden frowned, shifting Justin on her knee into an upright position, his little face held between her thumb and finger as her other hand rubbed his back.

'Christmas.' Nick said with a note of exasperation, as if the conversation they had had a few hours ago should still be at the front of her mind.

'I'll sort something out,' Eden said airily. 'Though I have to admit I'm not particularly looking forward to ringing my parents tonight and telling them I'm not coming home.'

'Will they be upset?'

'Not upset.' Eden shook her head. 'Just sorry, I guess, and worried that I'll be on my own.'

'But you don't have to be on your own,' Nick said, and Eden just shrugged and turned her attention back to the babe in her arms, continuing to rub his back in an attempt to bring up the wind she was sure was there. 'Why don't you spend it with me and my family?'

Despite a very loud burp from a very little baby, Eden carried on rubbing his back, determinedly not looking at up as her cheeks started to colour, waiting for Nick to roar with laughter or make some wisecrack to show that he was joking, but when finally she did jerk her eyes up to look at him, she was shocked to see that his face was deadly serious.

'It makes perfect sense,' Nick insisted. 'My sister's kids are spending the day with their dad and they won't be there till the evening so there won't be any tantrums, and my mum's an amazing cook so you can have the massive roast dinner you're dreaming of. At least you can tell your parents when you ring them that you're not going to be on your own.'

'And what's in it for you?' Eden asked directly, her eyes narrowing as Nick blushed slightly.

'I just don't like the thought of you being on your own,' Nick attempted, but Eden just slowly shook her head.

'What's in it for you, Nick?' she asked again.

'Well, if I hinted to Mum that we were seeing each other, I guess that would buy me a few months of grace.'

'You mean get them off your back?'

'Something like that. Think about it, Eden. It would be good for both of us and you'd have a great day, I can guarantee it.'

'So why not ask one of your many admirers? I'm sure Tanya's hoping for an invitation to meet your family.'

'Exactly.' Nick rolled his eyes. 'I spoke to her last night and unfortunately you're right— she was hoping...' He gave an embarrassed shrug. 'Suffice to say an invitation to Tanya to spend Christmas with me and my family could only confuse things, whereas with you and I...' He gave another shrug. 'Well, we'd both know that there was...'

'Nothing in it,' Eden finished for him as his voice trailed off. 'Thanks but, no, thanks.'

'Why not?'

Somehow she managed a smile as she placed a nappy over her shoulder and rested Justin against it as she stood up.

'Playing your girlfriend for a day, just isn't my idea of a fun Christmas,' Eden said. Heading down the ward and coming to Justin's room, she pushed the door open. 'You'll have to come up with someone else, Nick.'

'Think about it,' Nick said, but Eden shook her head.

''Night, Nick.'

As the door closed behind her, she placed Justin in his cot, soothing him gently as he struggled to open his heavy eyes. She listened to the sound of Nick's footsteps going down the ward and felt the sting of a great salty tear as it rolled down her cheek.

Stupidly, she'd dreamed of that very moment.

Secretly dreamed of Nick asking her to be with him and his family, the thought of sharing Christmas with him a fantasy she'd harboured—only not like this.

Never like this.

CHAPTER THREE

'SHE'LL never agree.' Becky shook her head as Eden wrestled with six feet four of hulking pine tree, dragging the beast the length of the nurses' station then levering it up to its full height. 'Donna *always* has it on the far side of the nurses' station.'

'Where no one can see it,' Eden retorted.

'Where it doesn't get in the way,' Becky countered with a grin. 'She'll have a fit when she sees that you've moved it.'

'Then she shouldn't have asked me to sort out the Christmas decorations, "given that the ward's so quiet".' Eden's rather purse-lipped impression of her senior rapidly faded as Becky gave a quick cough and started shuffling a pile of papers in front of her. Eden sucked in her breath as Donna Adams arrived at the nurses' station with a mountain of empty boxes. She was clearly not in the least impressed with what she was seeing.

'*What,* may I ask, is the tree doing there, Sister?'

'I thought it was more visible,' Eden attempted. 'That more of the children would be able to see it from their beds.'

'It's in the way,' Donna clipped. 'This is a hospital, Eden, not the local shopping centre. If, or rather when, there's an emergency the staff have enough to deal with, without manoeuvring crash carts around a blessed tree.'

'But there's plenty of room.' Eden stood firm, determined not to back down, determined for once in her life to stand up to Donna. 'I've measured it. And, yes, this is a hospital, but it's also a children's ward—'

'Nice tree!' Nick announced, depositing a mug of coffee and smothering a yawn, clearly oblivious to the argument that was taking place. 'When are the decorations going up?'

'Once Sister Hadley moves it back to the

other side of the nurses' station,' Donna said tartly, and as Nick's eyes darted between the two women, Eden saw a twist of a smile on his lips as he picked up on the tension. 'I was just explaining that the reason we keep it at the far side of the table is that in the event of an emergency we need to be able to manoeuvre the trolleys—'

'There's plenty of room,' Nick broke in. 'They're not supermarket trolleys, Donna, we do have some control over them.'

'But the patient files are kept there.'

'Then move them,' Nick responded. 'It's much better here—more of the kids can see it.'

Given that Nick was the consultant, the argument was effectively over, but Donna wasn't particularly gracious in defeat, thrusting a pile of empty boxes in Eden's direction. 'You can wrap these for under the tree, and I do not want to come in tomorrow morning to mountains of tinsel and fake snow over all my windows and plastic Santas stuck to the wall. Could we try and aim for tasteful?'

'Children and tasteful don't exactly mix,'

Eden muttered, but only when Donna was safely halfway down the corridor and heading for home! 'What is her problem?'

'She just likes to remind everyone she's the boss,' Nick answered, scribbling furiously on some notes and not looking up as he spoke. 'She's a honey really.'

'Only because *you're* the real boss.' Becky grinned, leaning over and peering down the corridor to make sure Donna really had left before rummaging in her wicker basket under the desk. She pulled out a container and shovelled a delectable-looking slice of cake on a paper towel and placed it beside Nick's mug. 'Here you go, Nick, have some chocolate cake with your coffee. 'Eden?' she offered, but Eden shook her head.

'Not for me, thanks. I'd better get on with this tree, given that I'm going to be seeing so much of it.'

'Oh, Eden, I am sorry about that, but it wasn't just for me that I said no.'

'I know,' Eden admitted. 'It's hardly fair on Conner as you worked last year.'

'It's not just Conner who'd be upset.' Becky let out a low sigh. 'I don't think Hamish would have taken it too well if I'd had to tell him that I was going to be working. Believe me, his tantrums lately are worse than anything Conner can pull off.'

Eden carried on listening to Becky's woes as she climbed onto a footstool, unraveling a bundle of fairy lights as she did so. She felt horribly self-conscious all of a sudden, acutely aware of Nick just a few metres away. Not that he was paying any attention, Eden consoled herself, tugging down her dress with one hand as she reached up to the top of the tree with the other and started draping the lights—he was too wrapped up in his notes.

'You should check them first.' Nick's voice caught her unawares and she swung around too quickly, embarrassed but grateful that, almost like a reflex action, he reached out his arm to steady her. 'Careful, Eden,' he warned, and Eden was grateful for the semi-darkness, which meant that Nick couldn't see her blushing, which she was—furiously. His fingers tightened around her wrist. 'Do you want me to do it?'

'Do what?' Eden blinked, her mind having wandered well away from the subject.

'To check the lights for you,' Nick explained patiently. 'Before you go to all the trouble of decorating the tree, first you ought to plug them in to make sure they're working.'

'Oh, Nick!' Eden simpered. 'What on earth would we do without you?'

'That's why he's a doctor,' Becky said in a proud, village-idiot type of voice, and Nick started to realize he was being teased. 'Because he's so clever.'

'I was only trying to help.' Nick moaned, finally getting around to his coffee and cake. 'I'll keep my mouth shut next time.'

'Please.' Eden grinned, resuming the difficult task as Nick picked up his cake and eyed it greedily.

'I've just realised that I'm starving.'

'Well, enjoy.' Becky smiled. 'Eden didn't want any so there's another piece here if you fancy it.'

Quite simply, Eden couldn't resist it. Still on the footstool, the fairy lights poised in her hand, she turned her head to watch Nick's face as he took a bite of the moist chocolate sponge and Becky pushed the container holding Eden's slice towards him. 'Help yourself, Nick.'

It was sheer poetry in motion. Nick closed his eyes, just as one did when one was about to sink teeth into something divine. Eden watched as he took a very generous bite of the chocolate cake and then witnessed his eyes snapping open. The public school system had certainly done its job when they'd taught young Nicholas his manners because his moan of horror turned in an instant to a groan of approval.

'What ingredients do you use, Becky,' Eden asked innocently, turning her attention to the tree and smothering a smile, 'to get it so moist?'

'Tofu,' Becky smiled. 'Though I swear a good soy milk helps—none of that genetically engineered rubbish. And Hamish has found a store that does the most delectable vegan chocolate chips. I'm going to make one of those for

Christmas—this was just a practice run. You will come,' Becky checked, jumping up as a buzzer went off. 'I'll get it.'

'What the hell is it?' Nick choked, using the paper towel Becky had thoughtfully provided but for a reason she had never intended!

'It's awful, isn't it?' Eden giggled. 'All her food's the same. It looks fantastic, but when you taste it. Don't!' Eden yelped as Nick went to toss the rest of his cake in the waste-paper basket. 'She'll see. Use the sharps bin.'

'I gather that you've done this before,' Nick said in a loud whisper, shoving the remains into the sharps bin, which had a closed lid that hid the contents from sight.

'Many times,' Eden admitted.

'You absolutely cannot go there for Christmas. It's no wonder Conner and Hamish are throwing tantrums if that's what Becky's trying to feed them!'

'What can I say to her?' Eden giggled again. 'She knows that I can't get home and, given she was there when I found out, it's not as if I can pretend I've got other plans.'

'You could have,' Nick reminded her, but thankfully her pager bleeped, giving Eden an excuse not to get into the uncomfortable topic. Glancing down at her neon yellow pager, the numbers displayed were instantly recognisable as Accident and Emergency. As Eden was the admitting nurse for the paediatric unit that evening and all admissions had to come through her in order to be allocated, it could only mean one thing—a new admission was on the way.

'Eden Hadley, admitting nurse for Paeds,' Eden said as she was connected, listening to an unfamiliar nursing sister and scribbling down an initial diagnosis as Nick looked on. 'Chest infection or difficulty feeding.' She shared a wry grin with Nick as Emergency attempted to shuffle their patient to the top of the list. 'And he's three years old. Have we had him before?'

An incredibly long wait ensued as the nurse attempted to locate the patient's history, reeling off a long list of complaints until finally Eden halted her.

'Ben!'

'No,' came a hesitant voice down the line. 'The name I've got is Maxwell Benjamin Reece, he's a three-year-old with Down's syndrome. He's also…' The nurse lowered her voice and Eden rolled her eyes, finishing the sentence for her.

'HIV positive. He's familiar to the ward, but he goes by the name of Ben. Could you let the staff who are dealing with him know that, please? Who's with him?'

The frantic scribbling on her notepad had stopped—Ben was familiar to anyone who worked on the paediatric unit and Eden didn't need to write down his past history. She gave a frown as the emergency nurse cheerfully declared that he had come in accompanied by Lorna, a social worker. It became clear that, yet again, little Ben was a ward of the state, that he'd had a chest X-ray and that they wanted to send him up soon as they were getting pretty full. Maybe it would be better if he was in familiar surroundings.

'Send him straight up,' Eden said, replacing the phone in its cradle.

'Ben?' Nick checked.

'Minus his new foster-parents.' Eden ran a hand through her hair, pulling out her tie and collecting all the loose curls that had fallen out and replacing them, an automatic gesture she did ten, maybe twenty times a day,

'What's the diagnosis?'

'They're fumbling to get one.' Eden gave a tight smile. 'Why don't they just admit that little Ben's too much like hard work?' Closing her eyes for a moment, she instantly regretted her words. It wasn't for her to judge. Ben wasn't just her favourite patient. Everyone, from cleaner to consultant, adored Ben, but, as cute as he was, he had been dealt more than his fair share in life. Genetic, social and hereditary problems seemed to have aligned when he had been conceived. 'I'm just sick of seeing him passed around, Nick. It just doesn't seem fair that one little boy should have to put up with so much.'

'He's happy,' Nick said soothingly.

'Is he?' Eden wasn't so sure. 'He just doesn't

know any better, Nick. He's never been given a chance.'

And though no one could have expected a drug-addicted teenage mum to deal with a Down's syndrome baby, if Ben's mum had only revealed her pregnancy earlier than in the labour ward, had received antenatal care and been diagnosed as HIV positive, then she could have taken some measures that could have lowered the chances of her transmitting the disease to her son. Sophisticated antiretroviral drugs could have been given during pregnancy and labour, even in the period following birth, but Ben had received none of these. Only when his mother's results had come back ten days post-birth had her HIV status been revealed, and despite the best preventative treatment her HIV status had been passed on to her son. As the weeks had dragged by into months, as endless foster-parents had tried and failed, little Ben was constantly returned to the hospital. It would seem that hospital was the only home this little boy knew. But Nick seemed to understand how Eden was feeling.

'Someone will come along soon for him.'

'When?' Eden asked, not even attempting to hide the bitterness in her voice. 'He's not going to live long, Nick—you and I both know that. I just really hoped...' She didn't finish, couldn't, tears stinging her eyes.

'Really hoped what?'

'That he'd get one Christmas with a family, that this foster-placement would work out...' Eden choked, 'One Christmas of being of spoilt and cuddled, one Christmas being loved...'

'Ben doesn't go short of cuddles,' Nick pointed out, 'All the staff love Ben. He'll get all that here.'

Eden shook her head. 'Twenty-eight kids will get that here, Nick—the nurses will make sure of it—but most kids that are here over Christmas are here because they're very sick. We're stretched to the limit normally, but especially over Christmas. Most of the children will have parents and siblings, aunties and uncles to dote on them, and Santa will come and visit. We'll do our very best for Ben, but no matter how hard we try it's not the same as...' she took a deep breath '…a family Christmas. As much as you mock it, Nick, as much as we all grimace sometimes at the thought of it, we wouldn't have it any other way. And that little guy has never had it, not even once.' Eden shook her head, more to clear it. She couldn't allow herself to get so involved, it wasn't healthy for anyone. 'I'd better go and get a cot ready—he's already on his way up.'

One look at those big brown eyes and Eden was instantly reminded why Ben was everyone's favourite—it wasn't just sympathy for his ailments that evoked such a response, it was all to do with a little guy who could melt the hardest heart at fifty paces. His dark hair was a wild mop around his little face, his almond-shaped eyes were always expressive, and his cute mouth broke into a wide grin despite the bottle he was halfheartedly sucking on as Eden greeted him.

'Hey Ben, we've missed you!'

'*Den!*' Ben answered, and Eden was thrilled that he remembered her name. He'd only just started to talk a few weeks ago when he'd last been admitted as a patient, and *Den* had been one of his early words, *more* being near the top of the list.

More milk.

More chocolate.

More cuddles.

But his first word had been the one that had torn at Eden. Whereas most children started their vocabulary with a gummy *mum* or *dada,* Ben's first word had been *no.*

No to the endless drips and IVs, *no* to the mountain of medicine he had to take and, saddest of all, *no,* when his favourite nurses' shifts ended and they popped in to say goodnight.

Lifting him up off the trolley, Eden expertly negotiated the oxygen tubing and carried him to his freshly made-up cot. She propped Ben up on a couple of pillows she had prepared so that he remained semiupright to allow for greater chest expansion and strapped an oxygen saturation probe to his fat foot. There was no murmur of protest. Ben was way too used to the procedure to fuss, as most toddlers would have.

'I'm just going to speak to the nurse and then I'll be back, Ben.'

The nurse giving handover didn't have much more information to give than she'd had over the telephone. 'He's reluctant to take fluids and mildly dehydrated and his ears are clear. But he wasn't about to let us look down his throat…'

'Typical Ben.' Eden smiled, knowing how much Ben hated having his throat examined. 'Why hasn't he got an IV?'

'The doctor thought we should rehydrate him via a nasogastric tube first.'

'But he hasn't got one in,' Eden pointed out.

'We tried to put it down but he got very distressed. We're trying him with his bottle.' The nurse didn't quite meet Eden's eyes as she answered and even before her next question came, Eden already knew the answer.

'Has he been given any antibiotics?'

'Oral,' the nurse said, pointing to the prescription chart. 'He's only got a mild infection—this admission seems more social.'

Lorna, the social worker, gave a murmur of agreement. 'The family just couldn't cope.

We're going to have to look for some alternative type of placement. Ben's just proving too hard to place with a family. His medical needs are so time-consuming and behaviourally he's very demanding as well…'

'Because he's confused,' Eden argued futilely. 'Once he settles into a routine he's fine. Look how good he is here.'

'I know,' Lorna sighed. 'But it's looking more and more likely that Ben's going to end up in a residential unit—there aren't many foster-families out there capable of looking after a child with Ben's needs. I'll speak to Donna first thing tomorrow and pencil in a team meeting for the end of this week. We really do need to look at some other options for Ben.'

'Donna?' The emergency nurse asked.

'She's the paediatric unit manager,' Eden explained as she took the admission notes and X-ray films, her heart sinking at the thought of Ben living out his short life in a long-stay residential facility. 'As you can probably tell, we all know Ben pretty well. What bloods have been done?'

'None.' The emergency nurse gave a rather too casual shrug. 'It was a locum and he's not used to taking blood from a child. He thought it might be better for Maxwell, I mean Ben, if the paediatrician did it on the ward.'

It would have been easier to say nothing, to just take the notes and say goodbye, but Eden simply couldn't just walk away.

'Did you remind the doctor about universal precautions?'

'I'm sorry?' Confused, the nurse frowned back at her.

'Did you remind the doctor that every patient, regardless of their symptoms or status, should be treated as if they have a communicable blood disease?'

'I don't know what you mean,' the nurse said, but from the colouring in her cheeks she clearly did.

'We *know* Ben's HIV positive,' Eden said tersely. 'Remind the doctor for me that it's the patients we don't know about that should cause us the most concern.'

'Eden.' As the emergency nurse stormed off,

Lorna touched her arm. 'Don't go getting upset.'

'Why don't they just admit that they didn't want to put an IV in, rather than coming up with all that nonsense about pushing fluids and the doctor wasn't used to taking blood from children? What the hell's he doing a shift in Emergency for? It's a cop-out and everyone knows it!'

'Just who are you really cross with here, Eden?'

'Don't try your psychobabble on me, Lorna,' Eden said, running a worried hand over her forehead. 'Do you really think he's going to end up in residential care?'

'He might,' Lorna said warily. 'Look, Eden, there's nothing you can do. We've been over and over the options and there's just no way that you can manage—'

'Manage what?' Nick's voice had both women jumping, and Eden shot an urgent look at Lorna as Nick frowned at the two of them, clearly expecting to be brought swiftly up to date.

'We were just discussing Ben's long-term care,' Lorna said warily. 'Discussing his options.'

'And what exactly is it that Eden can't manage?' Nick asked, his question direct, his eyes swinging between the two women who were both taking great interest in the floor all of a sudden.

'Nothing,' Eden mumbled. 'I was just moaning about the staff in Emergency, how they didn't take any blood or put in an IV. Lorna just pointed out there was nothing I could really do to change things, that technically they'd done nothing wrong.' A lousy liar at the best of times, Eden scuffed the floor with her foot, only letting out a relieved breath when Nick, clearly not impressed, stalked off.

Eden looked anxiously at Lorna. 'You won't say anything?'

'Why would I?' Lorna shrugged. 'You've done nothing wrong.'

'Thanks.' Eden gave a tense nod. 'It's just if anyone found out, they'd think…'

'That you were too involved?' Lorna finished for her. 'Which you are, Eden.'

'I can handle it,' Eden said stiffly, but Lorna didn't look particularly convinced.

'You know my pager number—if you need to talk any time, call me.'

Nick was already midway through his examination by the time Eden arrived at the cot-side. She smiled down at Ben as Nick gently probed his abdomen.

'Could you hold him for me while I check his ears and throat?' Nick asked.

Eden happily obliged. She picked Ben up and took a seat, holding his head against her chest as Nick carefully checked one ear and then deftly turning Ben around so that the check could be repeated on the other side.

'Now for the fun bit,' Nick said in a dry tone.

Eden held Ben tightly, one hand clamped on his forehead, as Nick attempted to check his throat. But this was the part Ben hated. Instantly he clamped his jaws tight, shaking his little head furiously as Nick waited with his lolly stick and torch poised for when he finally gave in and opened his mouth.

'Come on, buster,' Nick coaxed. 'It's only going to take a second.'

And as Ben finally gave in, his mouth opening in a sob of fury, Nick pushed down his tongue and peered down his throat. Ben squealed his protests and Eden waited, waited for the cursory examination to be over, for the torch to flick off and for Nick to throw the lolly stick into the plastic bag, but instead Nick was pushing the stick harder. Ben gagged and Eden's knuckles were white as she struggled to hold his head still. Nick peered around the child's mouth. For an appalling second Eden thought she might let go, that she might just rip that blessed lolly stick out of Nick's hand, might tell him to stop looking for things that she didn't want him to see.

But she didn't.

Instead, she held Ben firmly, fear—pure, naked fear—growing in the pit of her stomach. Cold fingers of terror touched her heart as Nick finally pulled out the lolly stick, but instead of taking Ben from her as he always did, instead of comforting the sobbing child, he pulled off his gloves and gently probed the little boy's neck, his fingers working their way slowly down to his axilla.

'Lay him on the cot for me.'

Nick's voice was flat, his eyes not meeting Eden's as she did as she was told. She watched as he pulled off Ben's nappy and carefully examined his groin.

'He's a bit dehydrated. We should put in a drip and do some bloods.'

'I can try and give him a bottle. Maybe once he's settled…' She stopped talking as Nick almost angrily shook his head.

'He isn't drinking because his mouth is sore,' he explained. 'He's got oral candida.' Children the world over got thrush—there were two babies on the ward at this very minute with the same condition—but the huge difference was that Ben was three years old and was HIV positive, and thrush was one of the warning signs in a child like Ben that his condition could be tipping over into full-blown AIDS. 'He's got enlarged lymph nodes, Eden.' Nick's voice bordered on the apologetic, as if the news he was delivering was somehow his fault. 'And from his notes he's lost weight since his last admission. We need to do a full lab screen and see exactly where we are.'

The treatment room was the place of choice for performing procedures. Any child upset on the ward made the other children anxious and where possible patients were moved to the treatment room well out of earshot of the other children. Even though Ben's skin would be numbed, the insertion of an IV and taking of blood was distressing for a small child, especially one like Ben who, even if he couldn't feel it, knew exactly what was happening and his tears and distress would upset the other children on the ward. But Ben had passed through the doors many times and Eden felt him stiffen in her arms as she carried him along the corridor. 'It's OK, sweetheart,' Eden said softly. 'Dr Nick's just going to fix you up with a drip so we can make you feel better very soon. He'll be very gentle.'

They worked well together. Eden held the reluctant toddler firmly as he bucked and struggled to get off the treatment bed, one hand gripping his arm tightly as Nick attempted to bring up a vein. She talked to Ben all the while, smiling down at him as Nick cut up tape, knowing full well that IV access in a child had to be secured very firmly if a repeat procedure was to be avoided.

'I'm in,' Nick said, but Eden didn't move, just held on tightly to Ben while Nick secured the bung then put an arm splint in place, immobilising Ben's little arm and then applying a huge bandage.

'Leave a gap,' Eden reminded Nick, because the IV site needed to be checked regularly to ensure that the line was patent and there were no signs of infection.

'Done.'

Only when Nick had said that word did Eden relax. At that point a child would normally be handed to his parents for a well-earned cuddle and Eden was more than happy to fill in, but

Nick did the honours, scooping up his patient and holding him firmly.

'I'm sorry, Ben, but that nasty old drip is going to make you feel much better soon.'

His clipped public school voice was supremely gentle and his firm grip still tender. Eden watched as Ben relaxed under Nick's touch, the exhausting day catching up with him. His sobs became less urgent, fading into a hum, each blink of Ben's eyes lengthening in time as Nick cuddled him to sleep.

'He's going to sleep,' Nick said. He didn't lower his voice but kept it steady. Most babies were soothed by background noise, comforted by an adult presence, but Ben in particular was more than used to the constant hum of a busy hospital ward.

'Keep on doing what you're doing, Nick. Ben's almost impossible to get to sleep. I'll go and prepare his cot and set up the IVAC. You've got time?' she checked, knowing a lot of doctors didn't list rocking babies in their job description.

'I'll make time,' Nick said, not looking up,

just holding the little guy tight. Eden had anticipated his answer—Nick's patients came
first always.

Of course, as soon as they laid him down,
Ben awoke and, despite his sore throat,
screamed loudly, his face purple as he simul-
taneously coughed and wept. All Eden could
do was hold his hand and rub his forehead. She
willed sleep to arrive for him so that his tortu-
ous day would be over, but again and again Ben
fought sleep. Every time Eden thought he was,
and attempted to slip out of the room and check
on the rest of her patients, Ben would break
into distraught sobs, his oxygen saturation
dropping markedly as he vomited.

'Should you give him something to settle
him?' Eden asked, watching anxiously as
Becky and Rochelle ran the length of the ward.
She knew that she really ought to be out there,
helping.

'I'd rather not when all he wants is a cuddle.'
Nick let out a weary sigh, but suddenly his
voice brightened. 'I've got an idea. Wait here!'

As if she had a choice!

Turning her attention back to Ben, Eden offered him his soother again, gently pushed him back down on the pillow, feeling resistance in every muscle. But suddenly he relaxed, the soother in his mouth slipping as his red, chafed face broke into a smile that could only be described as wondrous.

'Hey!' Eden grinned back. 'What do you see, little guy?' Turning around, following Ben's gaze, a smile broke out on her own face as she stared at the still crudely decorated Christmas tree, naked of tinsel and with the star at the top missing. But the lights she'd draped were turned on now, twinkling and flashing, and, Eden decided as Ben's sobs gave way to tiny whimpers, never had a tree looked more beautiful.

'See the lights,' Eden whispered. 'They're all little fairies, little fairies looking out for Ben…' She couldn't go on, the words that normally came so easily as she soothed a distressed child off to sleep just too hard to say tonight. The words stuck in her throat as she wrestled with her tears, sniffing loudly and trying to smile down at the little boy.

But Nick was there now, tucking in the sheet around a now sleepy, docile Ben. Taking Eden's arm, he led her out of the room and into the first private available space, which happened to be the store cupboard.

'He's got full-blown AIDS, hasn't he?' Eden gulped, waiting, hoping for Nick to deny it.

Instead, he gave a tired shrug. 'We won't know that until the blood results comes back but, I have to admit, it doesn't look great.'

'It could just be a simple case of thrush, though,' Eden said hopefully. 'And just because—'

'Eden?' Nick broke in, his voice questioning, his eyes narrowing as he stared down at her, taking in the swollen reddened eyes, the trembling hands, her top teeth biting her bottom lip as she made an effort to keep from breaking down. 'Why don't I feel like I'm talking to Ben's nurse here? Why do I feel like I'm comforting a parent?'

'I'm allowed to be upset,' Eden retorted, pulling a tissue out of her pocket and blowing her nose. She pulled herself together and forced a smile. 'Look, I'm fine. It was just a bit of a shock, that's all. I really was expecting this to be a social admission. When you looked down his throat, I wasn't expecting you to find what you did. It just threw me.'

He continued to stare down at her, those green eyes taking in every flicker. She could smell the citrus tang of his aftershave, see the power in his arms, and for a second all Eden wanted to do was lean on him, to weep into his chest, to feel those strong arms comfort her, to have him tell her that it was all going to be OK, that little Ben was going to be fine.

But, quite simply, she couldn't, and, Eden realised, the horrible truth starting to sink in, neither could Nick say that Ben was going to be OK. So instead they stood there, for what seemed the longest time, Eden forcing a smile, pretending she could deal with this as Nick weighed up whatever was on his mind.

'We'll go for a drink when your shift's over.'

'A drink?' Bewildered, she stared back at

him. As friendly as they had once been, their relationship, if you could call it that, had never extended outside the hospital walls. A stupid flame of hope started to fizz in her stomach but instantly Nick doused it.

'Or we can talk tomorrow at work, in front of Donna, but I really think the conversation we're about to have should take place well away from the ward.'

'I'm in my uniform,' Eden protested.

'So?' Nick shrugged. 'We'll go to Kelly's over the road, you'll match everyone there!'

CHAPTER FOUR

NICK had been only half joking.

Kelly's was a favourite haunt for hospital staff and one Eden stayed away from. Sure, she'd been there for a couple of birthday celebrations and leaving dos, but generally she avoided it. Too many nurses waiting for too few doctors, there was a certain needy air to it that Eden didn't ever want to buy into. And her feelings about the place were only confirmed as she walked in with Nick. The crowded bar was filled with hospital personnel popping in after a late shift, but despite the fact it was crowded, despite the fact if Eden had walked in alone, no one would have turned a hair, as Nick walked in behind her, the atmosphere shifted suddenly. There was a buzz of expectation in the air and

Eden could have sworn half the women in the place suddenly seemed to suck in their stomachs and flick their hair. Curious glances were being shot in her direction as Nick guided her to a table at the back before going to get them both a drink.

Eden watched as he attempted to make his way to the bar. His name was called from several directions, groups dispersing as everyone suddenly decided that they too *needed* to go to the bar. Eden wondered for a moment what it would be like to be that beautiful, to have that effect on a crowded room. Could Nick really be blamed for taking his pick?

'Here.' Pushing a glass towards her, he smiled as she took a sip, watching her face screw up. 'Gin and lemon,' Nick said without apology. 'I thought you might need it.'

'If I'd wanted a gin, Nick, I'd have asked for it. I happen to be on an early tomorrow,' Eden snapped, feeling defensive.

'I'm not planning on getting you drunk and having my wicked way with you, Eden.'

Unfortunately! Eden gave a weak smile as the thought popped into her head.

'I'm worried about you.' As she opened her mouth to argue, Nick overrode her. 'I was actually worried about you during Ben's last admission. I spoke to Donna about it.'

'You spoke to Donna?' Appalled, she stared back at him. 'But why?'

'Because every shift you were looking after Ben.'

'It's called continuity of care,' Eden retorted. 'It's far better for Ben if he sees a familiar face.'

'But is it doing you any good?' Nick didn't back down an inch, confronting her angry stare with a firm one of his own. 'You're too involved, Eden.'

'I'm not.'

'So what were you talking to Lorna about this evening?' She could feel his eyes on her as she fiddled with her straw, took another sip of her beastly drink and tried to come up with an answer. 'If you won't tell me, Eden, I'll go and speak to her myself tomorrow.'

'Please, don't involve Lorna.' Instantly Eden shook her head.

'Then tell me.' Nick said simply, and as her hands shot up to her hair he reached for her wrist. 'Stop fiddling with that blessed hair-tie, Eden, and tell me what's going on.'

'Nothing's going on,' Eden said. 'I haven't done anything wrong.'

'I know that,' Nick said softly. 'Come on, Eden, tell me.'

His hand was still on her wrist. Her other hand fiddled with her straw and suddenly Eden was glad Nick had bought her a gin. She took a sip, feeling the sharp taste on her tongue, the warmth as she swallowed it causing enough of a mental diversion to stop the fresh batch of tears that she simply couldn't cry here of all places.

'Last time Ben was here, when we were having trouble placing him again,' Eden started, screwing her eyes closed, not sure how Nick was going to react, 'I asked Lorna about the possibility of arranging temporary guardianship for me. I wanted to be able to take Ben out

now and then.' She couldn't look up, could feel Nick's hand tighten around her wrist. She could maybe have got away with leaving it there, but she knew Nick was too shrewd to accept half a story, that, no doubt, he'd follow it up and find out the whole truth anyway. Despite her reluctance to tell him, as she tentatively continued, there was also a feeling of relief, an unburdening as she finally told Nick the truth. 'Lorna wasn't keen, she gave the same warnings about getting too involved, but when I spoke to her properly, told her that it wasn't just about Ben, it was something I'd always wanted to do, she was really helpful.'

'Is it something you've always wanted to do?' Nick checked, and Eden nodded.

'My mum and dad are respite carers,' Eden explained. 'For as long as I can remember, once a fortnight or once a month we'd have some kid staying over, coming to the movies with us, perhaps to give their parents a break or, like Ben, to give them a break from the hospital. So I knew it was possible. Lorna gave me a lot of literature to read and part of it was about becoming a foster-parent. I thought you had to be married or a couple, certainly not a single working mum, but when I looked further into it, I realised that I actually fitted the criteria.'

'Oh, Eden.'

'Please, don't.' She put up a shaking hand, could hear the worried note in his voice. 'It isn't going to happen. If Ben were a normal healthy three-year-old, perhaps I could have managed it, but working shifts and everything, and with Ben's age and medical conditions, there was no way I could arrange child care while I worked. It was a complete non-starter. Still, I did go through the channels to become a respite carer, but by the time I'd been approved Ben had been allocated foster-parents.'

Her glass was empty now, and she didn't argue when Nick signalled to the bar staff for another round. She just managed a wry smile that Nick could manage waiter service in a packed bar and was grateful for the relative silence that followed as their drinks were brought over.

It was Eden that broke it.

'I suppose you're going to tell me I'm too involved,'

'I don't have to, Eden. I'm sure you already know that.'

Eden nodded.

'We have to maintain a professional distance.'

'I do,' she choked. 'Or I have. I know that we're not supposed to get too close and in ten years of nursing I never have. Sure, I get upset when a child's very sick or dies, everyone does, but till now it's been part of the job, a horrible part perhaps, but I could still see the bigger picture. It's just with Ben, I don't feel there's anyone really pulling for him, there's no one in his corner, fighting for him.'

'We all are,' Nick pointed out, but Eden shook her head.

'All he wanted tonight was a cuddle and, yes, he got one, but only for as long as the ward would allow it. I know that's just how it is, that as a nurse there's nothing I can do to change it. It's just…'

'Just what?'

'I adore him,' Anguished eyes met Nick's and

she watched as he flinched. 'I'm supposed to feel guilty for even saying it.'

'You're crossing the line, Eden.'

'If I handed my notice in tomorrow and went off to some developing country to work with HIV-infected orphans, everyone would wish me well and tell me I was doing a great thing…' Nick frowned, clearly having no idea where she was heading. 'If I handed my notice in tomorrow to become a foster-parent for handicapped children, a few people might scratch their heads but again everyone would wish me well. But if, heaven forbid, I do it back to front, if I actually get attached to a patient who doesn't have anyone to call his own in the world, suddenly I'm crossing a line, suddenly I'm getting in too deep. We're supposed to care, but not too much, we're supposed to get involved in people's lives and still hold back.'

'We have to if we're going to stay sane.'

'But it's not a light switch, it's not something we can just flick on and off at will. We don't choose the people in our lives who are going to touch us. Sometimes, like it or not, it just happens…'

And something in her voice must have reached him because she felt the fight go out of him. A pensive look came over his face, his eyes softening slightly as he looked over at her.

'If you look after him, you're going to get hurt, Eden.'

'I know.' A brave smile wobbled on her lips. 'And if I don't look after him, if you stop me from being allowed to nurse him, then I'm going to get hurt even more.'

'Donna needs to know.'

'No!' Eden shook her head firmly, but Nick just stared right back.

'I can guarantee Donna's felt the same at some time in her career.'

'I doubt it.'

'I can guarantee it,' Nick said. 'And so have I.'

Her eyes jerked up to him.

'Lucy Wright, two years old with a cerebral tumour. I was a doing my paed internship and everyone, including my parents, told me it was just because I was young and relatively inexperienced, that it was because it was my first real experience with a terminally ill child, but even though I agreed with them to keep them quiet, the fact is, Lucy was just a great kid. I can still see her smile when I walked on the ward. She was blind,' Nick added, 'but she knew, just from my footsteps, that it was me. And, yes, I was young and relatively green and, yes, it was my first real experience with a terminally ill child, but I cried more than I ever have since over losing a patient when she died. Since then, to this day, I haven't cried that way again. And it wasn't just because she was two and that she didn't deserve it and that life wasn't fair. I cried, quite simply, because it was Lucy.

'We've all been there, Eden. That's why you need to tell Donna, so she can help you through it.'

'But Donna!'

'Yes, Donna,' Nick said firmly. 'That's why she's the unit manager, Eden. You've told me, so surely you can tell her.'

'Ah but I had two gins and a jukebox playing

in the background when I told you.' Eden smiled, but her heart wasn't really in it. With Nick it had been easy to open up, but with Donna it would be completely different. Eden just couldn't imagine telling the austere, immovable woman what was on her mind, let alone her actually understanding.

'I could talk to her for you,' Nick offered.

'You!' Eden said a touch ungraciously, but Nick just smiled.

'Yes, me, Eden. I am quite good at that sort of thing in case you haven't noticed.'

'Of course I have,' Eden said, chewing nervously on her bottom lip. 'If you do talk to her—I mean, if I do agree—you will tell her that I am capable of looking after Ben?'

'With support,' Nick said, and finally Eden agreed.

'With support.'

'Nick!' The falsely cheerful tones of Tanya, the orthopaedic intern, caught them both unawares. 'I haven't seen you in here for a while.'

'I've been busy,' Nick responded, barely even

bothering to look up, but his distinct lack of enthusiasm did nothing to deter Tanya.

'I was just going to the bar. Can I get you anything?'

'Not for me.' Nick shook his head and drained his glass. 'We were just leaving.'

'Really!' The smile was still in place but Tanya's eyes were distinctly frosty as she shot a look at Eden. 'Well, maybe next time, then.'

'Maybe not,' Nick said frostily. 'Come on, Eden.'

'Nick!' After the icy blast of the air conditioner the thick warm air was uncomfortable as they stepped outside. Eden could still feel the sting of her own blush as she swung to face him outside, their uncomfortable, rapid, exit from the pub hadn't been quite quick enough for Eden to miss the glitter of tears in Tanya's eyes and she was appalled at the way Nick had treated her. 'That was a bit harsh.'

'She'll get over it,' Nick said casually, and Eden shook her head, scarcely recognising the man who was standing in front of her. But Nick stood his ground. 'Eden, sometimes you have to be firm.'

'You don't have to be rude, though!'

'Maybe I do,' Nick said through gritted teeth. 'Just leave it, Eden.'

So she did, walking in uncomfortable silence along the street towards her home, still reeling from seeing a side to Nick she'd never thought she'd witness.

'What a difference a day makes,' Nick said, breaking the silence. 'This time yesterday you were furious that you had to work at Christmas, and now I bet you're just a little bit pleased.'

'A bit,' Eden admitted, but her mind was still whirling. The pain in Tanya's eyes had been real.

'You could have told me earlier you know, Eden,' Nick said as they arrived at the entrance to the town house she rented with Jim, who was clearly home and taking advantage of Eden's absence because the windows were practically vibrating to rock music. 'I mean, not just as a doctor but as a friend.'

'We haven't been friends for a long time,' In

the darkness she was somehow able to admit the truth. 'Not really. Sure, we talk about work and have a joke and that, but since Teaghan died...'

'It's been hard, Eden.'

'I know,' Eden answered. 'Well, I don't know exactly, but I can imagine. But you have to admit, Nick, things have changed. We haven't really been friends since Teaghan's death.'

'We were, though.' She couldn't see his expression in the darkness, but she could make out his profile, the hollows of his cheekbones as he stared down at her, the flash of his teeth as his mouth moved. 'We didn't know each other for very long before Teaghan died, but with some people I guess you just click.

'I've missed you Eden.'

His admission caught her completely unawares. There was a tiny raw note of urgency in his voice that she was too terrified to interpret, too scared of misreading the signs and making the biggest, most embarrassing mistake of her life.

'I've missed you too, Nick,' Eden answered

carefully. 'And I'm glad that we're talking again, glad that we're back to being friends.'

'Hey, Eden.' The front door swung open. Jim was standing in a pair of shorts and not much else, apart from a can of beer in hand, the thud-thud of his stereo spilling out onto the street. 'I was just putting the bins out.'

'And waking half the street,' Eden scolded. 'Since when did you put the bins out? Jim, this is Nick, he works at the hospital, Nick, this is Jim, my resident idle backpacker.'

'Who always pays his rent on time, though,' Jim answered cheerfully. 'Good to meet you, Nick. Fancy a cold one?'

'Not for me,' Nick answered, equally cheerfully. ''Night, then, Eden.'

''Night, Nick.'

There was a beat of a pause, a tiny moment of hesitation, and Eden wondered how to fill it. Suggest a coffee perhaps, say that she'd see him tomorrow…kiss him on the cheek even, just as a friend would, but Jim clattering past with the garbage bin completely broke the moment.

'I'd better get in,' Eden said, 'and turn down the music. I don't know why, but Jim has the uncanny knack of making me feel like a parent!'

'Really!' Despite the darkness she saw Nick's eyes widen. 'It seemed like the other way around to me.'

And, walking off, he left her frowning.

CHAPTER FIVE

IT WAS an incredibly shy Eden that walked onto the ward the following morning. She'd only had two drinks the previous night yet she felt as if she'd been at some wild party, the events pinging in and spinning her further into confusion—revealing the truth about Ben, Nick's behaviour towards Tanya and, strangest of all, that tiny moment at the end where she'd wondered if he might kiss her, or had it been, if she might kiss him?

'Good morning, Sister.' Donna was there, neat and trim, sitting on her office chair in the crowded handover room, queening it over everyone. Eden felt her heart sink at the prospect of what was undoubtedly to come later. 'Have a seat.' Pointedly Donna looked at her watch. 'We're just about to start. But before we do, we're expecting a new admission from Emergency—a two-year-old with rash and fever for investigation. She's also markedly dehydrated. I don't have her name just yet. Bruce, the registrar, has seen her in Emergency and she should be up soon—I've allocated Isolation room 2 for her. Right!' Donna nodded graciously to the night sister. 'Let's begin.'

The ward was pretty much as Eden had left it on her late shift, apart from a couple of admissions overnight from Emergency and ICU. A few of the patients were about to be discharged, which heralded a busy day for all. Discharges caused a lot of paperwork and no sooner had the discharge meds been given and the patient wheeled out of the ward then Emergency would be on the telephone, hoping to fill the freshly empty bed.

'Now.' Donna peered at her list. 'Does anyone have any preferences?' Turning in her chair, her sharp eyes swivelled around the room. On any other day, at this point Eden would have jumped right in, would have asked to take care of the isolation rooms, but, given that Nick would be talking to Donna later, Eden decided against it.

'I wouldn't mind having Bay 1,' Eden responded. 'I'd like to see how Priscilla goes with breakfast and lunch today.'

'Fine,' Donna agreed. 'You've got young Rory going to theatre for debriding of his wound—he's third on the orthopaedics list,' Donna reminded them. 'And Declan's being discharged now that his nausea and vomiting has finally stopped, so no doubt you'll have a new admission. And then you've got the new boy, Peter, going down for circumcision—he's second on the general surgeon's list.'

'And very hungry,' the night sister added. 'Hopefully they won't take too long with the first patient.'

'Now, I've got a management meeting at twelve, Eden,' Donna carried on. 'So if your bay's OK, can you take over from me then?' She didn't wait for Eden's response, turning instead to the rest of her team. 'OK, Rochelle, you can help Becky with the isolation…' As

Donna continued allocating duties, Eden stayed, initialling each patient on her list with the nurse that was looking after them, so that if there were any enquiries or drugs to be checked, Eden would know who to go to.

'She's in fine form this morning,' Becky whispered as they made their way out of the office. 'Must have had her Prozac!'

'I hope she took two,' Eden responded.

'Meaning?'

'I'll tell you later.'

'How come you didn't take the isolation rooms?' Becky asked, pulling a stethoscope off the rack on the wall and grabbing a tympanic thermometer.

'I'll tell you that later, too.'

She hadn't expected to see Nick so soon. Even as Eden entered the bay and saw the curtains drawn around Priscilla's bed, she figured seven-thirty a.m. was a bit too early for Nick. But then again…

Seeing his highly polished shoes beneath the curtain, Eden allowed herself the indulgence of a quick cringe, burying her burning face in the mountain of linen she'd piled onto her trolley in preparation to make the beds. But she'd forgotten her audience and instantly regretted her actions as a thoroughly bored Rory decided to ask what exactly her problem was!

'Are you feeling sick, Eden?'

'Cool,' Declan responded. 'She's going to faint.'

'I'm fine,' Eden said quickly. 'I'm just checking that I've got enough linen.'

'In case you've wet the bed,' Declan teased Rory.

'In case you've been sick…' Rory answered back.

'Enough,' Eden snapped, heading for the television, but Rory called her back.

'We're not allowed to watch it until *Princess* has had her breakfast.'

'Her name's Priscilla,' Eden said as her finger recoiled from the 'on' button. Heading for her trolley, she peeled off a gown and some towels. 'OK, Rory, I'll get you a bowl and you can have a wash and then I'll come and help you into a gown for Theatre, but first I'm just going to check on Priscilla…'

'Morning.' Nick appeared from behind the curtain. Unlike Eden, he was utterly together, his newly washed blond hair, still damp from the shower, flopping over his forehead as he stared down at Priscilla's chart, his aftershave, his suit, his presence just a sheer, delectable notch above the rest. 'Can I borrow you, Eden?' He gestured and Eden duly headed out of the bay.

'How is she?'

'Fine.' Nick gave a half-laugh. 'Or at least she will be soon.'

'I'm not with you.'

'I've listened to her stomach and there are a few rumblings. I'm expecting the train in at any moment!'

Even Eden managed a laugh. 'So the veggies are working?'

'Priscilla isn't going to know what's hit her. I'll come and check on her later this afternoon. If she's still in pain I'll have to order another abdo X-ray, but I'm pretty sure we can avoid it. I think she'll be feeling a lot better soon.

'How are you?' he added, shifting the conversation to the personal.

'Fine,' Eden gulped.

'Good.'

The conversation would have continued, but at that point a rather frantic-looking Priscilla appeared at the curtains and Eden knew from the rather pained expression on the little girl's face that this conversation would have to take place later.

'This way, Priscilla.' Eden smiled as the little girl bustled past. 'I'll be with you in a moment. And, remember, don't flush till I've been in.' She turned to Nick. 'I think the train's just pulling in.'

'About time,' Nick answered, stepping out of the way as Eden ducked past.

'How are you doing Priscilla?' Eden asked, knocking on the bathroom door a good fifteen minutes later. As the lock slid open and a pale-faced Priscilla peered out, Eden decided that if anyone thought nursing was glamorous, they clearly hadn't read this part of the job description.

'Not very well.'

Priscilla looked as if she were about to faint as Eden let herself in.

'On the contrary.' Eden somehow grinned, pushing the flush button. 'In fact, Priscilla, I'd say life's just about to get a whole lot better for you!'

Eden walked Priscilla back to her bay and as the little girl went to climb back into bed, Eden instead suggested she sit in the chair to have breakfast. Not leaving any room for argument, Eden started to strip the bed.

'I'll give you some nice fresh sheets. Oh, here comes breakfast now.'

Priscilla didn't look particularly impressed with her cereal and fruit but at least she didn't throw it on the floor this time. Instead, she ate it with a pained expression at each mouthful, which Eden pointedly ignored as she guided Declan towards the showers.

'Your mum should be here soon for the doctors' round.'

'And then I'll be going home?' Declan said. 'I was only supposed to be in for the day.'

'It happens that way sometimes,' Eden said, turning on the taps for him and checking that he had soap, before putting out his toothbrush and paste. 'Now, give your teeth a good brush after your shower.'

'I know.' Declan, unlike some five-year-olds who expected you to do everything for them, was clearly waiting for her to leave before getting undressed.

'Have you got everything you need?'

'Yep.'

'Press the buzzer if you don't feel well…'

'I'll be fine.' Mr Independent shooed her out and Eden smothered a grin then headed off to the nurses' station to check all Rory's notes were ready for his trip to Theatre.

Rory had been knocked off his bike by a motorist three weeks previously. Thankfully he had been wearing a helmet which had, according to his notes, saved him from a serious head injury as he'd bounced, head first, off the car's windscreen. But his leg and pelvis hadn't fared quite so well. Rory had sustained a fractured right femur and shattered pelvis, along with a nasty degloving injury to his left thigh, which was requiring regular trips to Theatre for cleaning and debridement. This morning the orthopods were going to take a skin graft from his right thigh to cover the nasty wound and hopefully hasten healing.

Even though the night staff had assured her everything was ready, Eden double-checked. She was glad that she did—Theatre handover was not the best place to find out that something had been missed!

'Problem?' Donna asked briskly as Eden let out a moan.

'Professor Baines has written in the notes that he wants Rory to commence IV gentamycin *prior* to going to Theatre.'

'Then you'd better get on and give it,' Donna responded, then tutted loudly as Eden shook her head.

'It hasn't been prescribed.' Eden double-checked Rory's prescription chart then flicked through the notes in case a new one had been started. 'No, it's not written up anywhere.' Reaching for the phone, she paged the intern for Professor Baines's ortho team. 'The team is not going to be too thrilled,' Eden muttered. 'No doubt they're starting to scrub.'

Tanya certainly wasn't!

Tanya let it be known in no uncertain terms that this should have been picked up sooner, that the team was already scrubbed and about to start the list, but Eden wasn't in the mood for unnecessary dramas—it wasn't as if Tanya was going to be operating!

Holding the phone away from her ear, Eden gave an exaggerated eye roll as Tanya continued to moan.

'Look,' Eden said finally, 'I'm sorry it wasn't picked up earlier, but if you'd written up the prescription when Professor Baines gave his order, we wouldn't be having this conversation. Now, are you going to come and write it up?'

'Presumably that's a yes,' Eden said dryly as

the phone clicked off. Suddenly remembering Donna was present, Eden coloured up a touch, wondering if she'd sounded rude. 'She wasn't exactly helpful,' Eden said. 'She was blaming the ward…'

'When the mistake was hers,' Donna said through pursed lips. 'Good for you for standing up to her. And don't take any cheek when she comes up or *I'll* be having a word.'

If Tanya had been irritated before, when she flounced onto the ward a few moments later and put a name to the face that had been on the phone, she was seriously put out! Her usually pretty, elfin face scowled as she leant over the desk and scribbled on the prescription chart.

'This should have been picked up sooner,' she muttered, but Eden refused to rise to the bait, concentrating on paperwork of her own. 'Perhaps if the nurses on this ward weren't out till all hours…'

Eden shot her an appalled look, scarcely able to believe that Tanya could be so personal, so petty, but before she could think of a suitable retort Donna came up with one for her.

'I think that's quite enough, don't you, Doctor?' Donna's voice was pure ice. 'As Sister Hadley has pointed out, this was your mistake and just because the professor is giving you a hard time about having to leave Theatre, I'd suggest you learn from your mistake and move on.' She took a deep breath, positively withering Tanya with her eyes as the young intern flushed. 'And if you're referring to the fact that the consultant of this ward and one of my senior nurses were over at Kelly's last night, discussing a patient on this ward then, frankly, Doctor, my advice remains the same. Get over it and move on.'

'Ouch,' Eden winced as Tanya strode out of the ward. She turned shyly to Donna. 'Nick's obviously spoken to you.'

'He has.' Donna nodded. 'Let's get this gentamycin started and then we'll go into my office.'

Unlike Nick's office, Donna's was incredibly neat. Taking a seat behind her desk, she gestured for Eden to sit down, which Eden did, her heart hammering in her chest, her hands fidgeting in her lap. She wondered what on earth Donna was going to say—but it was actually Eden who spoke first.

'Thank you—for what you said to Tanya, I mean.'

'You're a member of my team, Sister,' Donna said, and Eden took a deep breath, knowing they were moving on now to the real reason they were there. 'I was actually already intending to have a talk with you about Ben before Nick spoke to me about it. I'd noticed how fond you were getting of him, how you always ask to look after him and that you often stay behind after your shift has ended.'

'I've never compromised his care.'

'Of course you haven't. Sister. You don't think that you're in trouble, do you?'

'I don't know,' Eden admitted. 'I feel as if I've done something wrong.'

'Eden.' Donna dropped her title. 'Behind that uniform you're a human being. That's why nurses will never be replaced by robots or machinery—it takes real people to do our job, and real people have real emotions. If Ben had a loving parent or even one relative who cared for him or came in and visited him, I know that you wouldn't be feeling this way—Ben would be one of your favourites, a patient you had a soft spot for, one that moved you more than most perhaps. But Ben doesn't have anyone. There's a huge gaping hole in this little boy's life and I can see how you might want to fill it.'

Of all the people she'd expected to understand, Donna had been the last, and Eden felt a sting of tears in her eyes as her senior spoke with more insight and compassion than Eden could have ever predicted.

'You know that my husband's paraplegic?' Donna asked, and Eden nodded. 'Do you know where I met him? I was nursing on a spinal unit,' Donna said, not waiting for Eden to answer. 'I was twenty-six years old and had worked on the unit for five years, since I'd qualified, and I loved every minute of it. We had the patients from the first day of their injury when they were transferred to us right through to when they moved to a small apartment while we prepared them for going home. I looked after David the whole way through and some-where along the way we fell in love.

'But that was twenty-five years ago. Not only did we have to deal with the scorn of my nurs-ing colleagues, but my parents were appalled too—they said that David was using me, that if he hadn't had his accident he'd never have even looked at me…' She smiled at Eden's ap-palled face. 'The reason I'm telling you this is that in those days there was no support—no one to talk to. I had to leave a job I loved as if I'd committed some sort of crime. Thankfully nursing's moved on a lot since then.

'Now!' Rather more crisply, Donna contin-ued. 'I've discussed this with Nick and we're both more than happy for you to look after Ben, with a couple of provisos.'

'Which are?'

'Firstly, and most importantly, if Ben col-lapses or his condition rapidly deteriorates, you're to summon help, make your patient safe and, so long as numbers allow, you're to step aside. I don't think it would be in either of your best interests to be involved in decision-making in an emergency situation.'

Eden nodded thoughtfully, actually relieved that that decision had been made for her.

'I'd like you to talk to me, weekly at least, so we can be sure how you're dealing with everything. If you don't feel you can discuss things with me, I can arrange—'

'That won't be necessary,' Eden interrupted. 'You've been really helpful.'

Donna gave a small nod. 'And finally, given that the paperwork has already been done with Social Services, I'm more than happy, so long as Ben's health permits, for you to take him out for short intervals—with the necessary precautions, of course—though not while you're on duty. If you take Ben off the ward it has to be as his carer, and therefore you'll need the doctor who's on call that day to come and assess Ben and approve him leaving.'

A sharp, familiar rap on the door ended the conversation. As the door opened, Eden didn't need to look up to know that it was Nick.

'Donna, sorry to interrupt. I've just been

speaking to a GP who wants to send a direct admission to the ward—a four-year-old who's just come back from overseas with query malaria. Can I use the last ISO room?'

'It's already taken.' Donna stood up. 'We're getting an admission from Emergency but ISO five is only in there because the parents demanded a single room.'

'I really do need it.'

'Then I'll tell the parents their child will have to move onto the main ward,' Donna said crisply. 'I warned them at the time this might happen.'

'How was it?' Nick asked as Donna bustled off. Instead of rolling her eyes, as was usually the case when Donna left the room, Eden found herself smiling.

'Good.' Eden blinked. 'Better than good. She was great. I can even take Ben out for short periods—if he's well enough, of course.'

And even though Nick smiled, somehow it didn't quite reach his eyes. His green eyes held hers for just a fraction too long, and she registered the tiny swallow in his throat.

'What is it, Nick?'

When he didn't answer straight away, Eden answered for him.

'His bloodwork's back, isn't it?'

Nick gave a hesitant nod, 'This isn't easy, Eden.'

'I know,' Eden whispered, because she did. In this very office, just a year ago, it had been Eden breaking bad news to Nick. Even though the circumstances were entirely different she knew how hard it was for him to be standing here now and hurting a friend because, just a year ago, she'd done it to him. Clearing her throat, Eden willed her voice to hold. 'What do his results show?'

'They're not all back yet and we'll need to do a lot more tests, but things aren't looking good for him. I've just been discussing his case with the infectious diseases consultant. As you know, Eden, it doesn't suddenly happen. AIDS is just what its name says: a syndrome. But un-fortunately Ben is starting to display some of the more obvious signs.' He paused for a mo-ment, allowed her to process the news before he gently continued. 'There are stages to this disease, Eden, and it looks as if Ben's HIV status has shifted.'

'He's going to die?'

'One day.' Nick nodded. 'And sooner than he deserves to, that's for sure. But with aggressive medication, with the right environment...'

'He's behind the eight ball already, then,' Eden rasped, choking back angry tears as Donna breezed back into the office.

'All sorted!' she said crisply. 'Eden, the orderly's here to take young Rory to Theatre.' Donna's sharp, knowing eyes swivelled between Eden and Nick. 'Is everything all right?'

'I was just discussing Ben's results with Eden,' Nick answered.

'I see.' Donna paused for a second before addressing Eden. 'Will you be OK to work, Eden?'

Eden nodded because, quite simply, she had to be. She couldn't afford the luxury of crying. Donna had offered her support through all this, but if Eden was going to break down whenever the news was bad for Ben, clearly things would have to be revised.

There would be time for that later.

'I'll be fine,' Eden said firmly, making her way out of the office and staring down the corridor she saw Ben through the massive glass windows of his ISO room. He raised a podgy little hand as he recognised her, his round face breaking into the widest of smiles as his beloved *Den* came into his view. Dragging in a deep breath, swallowing the tears that seemed to be choking her, somehow Eden managed to wave back, somehow she managed to give him a huge bright smile before heading back to her patients.

CHAPTER SIX

'WHERE'S Dad?'

Pulling open her front door, Eden blinked into the darkness, shocked to see Nick standing there, appalled that he should see her looking like this and confused at his question.

'Dad?'

'Jim,' Nick said, as if that should explain things, but when Eden just stared back at him, he explained further. 'Does he usually put the bins out?'

'Never.'

'Or stand on the street till you've waved off your friends?'

'Actually, yes…'Eden's mouth dropped open as a rather unwelcome penny dropped. 'Nick, you've got it all wrong. Jim and I are just housemates. He was just being…' Her voice trailed off, tiny seeds of doubt that had been sown over the past few weeks starting to sprout. 'Oh, that's all I need,' Eden murmured. 'Do you really think he likes me?'

'Take it from me.' Nick smiled. 'Where is he, then?'

'Gone to get some pizza.' Eden gave a tiny shrug. 'Trying to cheer me up.'

'Am I going to be asked in?'

'Sorry.' Pulling the door open wider, Eden stepped back. 'Of course.' She said it as if she meant it but really she'd have loved to slam the door in his face and dart upstairs for five minutes. Swollen red eyes weren't her only problem tonight. A scruffy pair of denim shorts and a halter top without the necessary accessory of a strapless bra wasn't exactly the look she was aiming for, at least not where Nick was concerned.

Stop it, Eden mentally scolded herself, padding along the floorboards in bare feet and showing Nick through to her unfortunately untidy lounge, reminding herself that Nick couldn't give a damn what she looked like on that level, he'd made that perfectly clear. She knew exactly why he was there.

'I assume you've come to check on me.' Sitting down on the sofa, Eden tucked her legs under her. 'To make sure that I'm *coping* with the news!'

'And are you?' Nick asked, ignoring her sarcasm. Bypassing the chair she'd assumed he's sit in, he sat himself down on the sofa beside her and Eden could feel him taking in her swollen eyes and reddened nose.

'Better now,' Eden admitted. 'I've had a good cry, thumped a few pillows. Jim's been great. It was my turn to cook but, as I said, he's insisted on going out and getting pizza. Do you want me to ring him,' she offered, 'and tell him to get some more? You're very welcome to stay.'

Nick shook his head. 'I'm actually on my way over to my parents'. I just wanted to see how you were doing.'

'Well, I'm fine,' Eden said in a rather falsely

bright voice. 'It was nice of you to think of me.'

'I had an ulterior motive.' Nick gave her the benefit of a rather devastating smile. 'I was rather hoping you'd had a rethink about Christmas. You've no idea how much easier my life would be if I could tell them I was bringing a date.'

'Nick!' Eden wailed, wishing he'd just drop it. She had enough to weep about tonight without this as well!

'Oh, well.' Nick shrugged. 'Nut roast for you, then!'

'Looks that way,' Eden sighed.

Nick stood up, and Eden did the same. Now he hadn't got what he'd obviously wanted, the conversation was clearly over.

As he reached the front door Nick turned around. "Would it change your mind if—?'

'Nothing will change my mind Nick.'

'Hear me out, Eden. How would you feel if Ben came with us?'

'Ben?' Her mood shifted from irritated to angry. It had been an emotional enough day without Nick using Ben as some kind of pawn. 'You'd use a three-year-old kid to get your way…'

'Hey!' Nick's single word halted her. 'I know you're upset, Eden, I know this has cut pretty deep for you, but for your information, I've been looking after Ben since the moment he was delivered. I resuscitated that little boy when he was born. It was me who diagnosed his Down's syndrome and it was me who opened an envelope one Monday morning and found out he was HIV positive. For three years I've been trying to save his life and today I've found out that it isn't going to happen—and as hard as it might be for you to deal with this, you're not the only one this news has affected.'

His outburst had her reeling, her own self-absorption shaming her now. He'd had to shout it for her to see it.

In his own way, Nick loved Ben—they all did.

'I'm so sorry.' Tears were close but she held them back, the sympathy card not one she wanted to play here.

'What you said the other day, when he was first admitted, about how you wished he could have just one Christmas, one day of being the centre of everyone's world…' Nick's eyes met Eden's, holding her gaze with possibility. 'We could give him that, Eden. Not a whole day perhaps, but for a couple of hours at least we could give Ben the Christmas he deserves. My parents were saying when I went over how much they're going to miss having the kids there at lunchtime, given Lily's divorce and everything. It would be so nice to have Ben with us, so nice to spoil him.'

'You'd really do that?'

'Of course,' Nick said, as if he was surprised she'd even had to ask. 'You can go home after your shift and grab a few hours' sleep, and once I've finished dishing out the presents at the hospital, I'll pick up Ben and come and get you.'

'Are you Santa this year?'

'I am.' Nick grinned. 'And I make a very fine one, too, even if I do say so myself. So what do you say?'

'And your parents will be OK, with his HIV status and everything?'

'They won't turn a hair.'

'There won't be any other kids there?' Eden checked. 'He shouldn't come into contact with any—'

'Hey.' Nick halted her again, only more gently this time. 'I'm a paediatric consultant, Eden.' He smiled at her embarrassed blush. 'So, can I tell my parents you're coming?'

'Yes.' Eden nodded, her first genuine smile of the day breaking out on her full mouth. 'Yes, please.'

Despite decorating the tree at work, despite the mountain of empty boxes she'd wrapped and placed around it, Christmas hadn't really seemed to be happening for Eden, but waking up the next morning, hearing a Christmas jingle on her alarm radio, the date caught up with her all of a sudden—seven days to Christmas and she hadn't done a thing.

Not a single thing!

'Oh, hell!'

Peeling back her sheet, Eden jumped out of bed and hit the floor running. She greeted a bleary-eyed Jim in the kitchen and gratefully accepted the coffee he poured.

'Who are you ringing?'

'The bank,' Eden groaned. She pulled her credit card out of her purse and keyed in the digits, hitting the hash key and keeping her fingers crossed as she listened for her available balance. 'If I post my prezzies today, do you think they stand a chance of getting there?'

Of course, first she had to buy them!

Her parents were easy to buy for, or at least predictable—for her father a CD of marching pipers which, Eden realised as she handed over her card for the first of many times that morning, at least she wouldn't have to hear this year, and for Mum a twelve-month supply of some impossibly expensive facial treatment that promised everything but coffee in bed in the morning!

On, ever on, until every last present for her family was wrapped and stuffed into a postpak and Eden queued up at the post office with the bulging box and a half-used roll of sticky tape that she still had to pay for, trying to fathom what on earth she should get for Ben and for Nick's family, given that they were having her for Christmas dinner. And, of course, for Nick himself! Over and over Eden had to quell her mounting excitement, over and over she had to replay Nick's rather harsh words to her. He'd told her there was nothing between them, had told her to her face that this was merely an exercise to get his parents off his back, but as she watched the shop assistant wrapping his present, she went the whole hog and added an extra two dollars to the bill to add a bow. Eden allowed herself the tiny indulgence of a daydream, imagined for a moment that this was how Christmas would always be.

'Who's the lucky bunny, going home?' Eden asked, walking into her allocated bay on the Ward, incredibly pleased to see Priscilla sitting on Rory's bed and playing a board game with him.

'Me.' Priscilla grinned, looking up from the

game. 'Dr Nick said I could go home this afternoon. Mum's finishing work early to come and get me.'

'Well, good for you,' Eden said as Priscilla turned her attention back to the game.

Picking up Priscilla's chart, Eden turned to the food chart that was being kept on the girl, checking off the contents of the tray and filling in what Priscilla had eaten. 'How did you go with lunch today?'

'OK.' Eden shrugged, not bothering to look up, and her nonchalance was the best reward of all. The fact she'd eaten a plate of steamed fish and vegetables and a bowl of jelly was just as it should be—no big deal.

'How are you doing, Rory?' Eden asked as Priscilla skipped off to the loo. She popped the tympanic thermometer in his ear and watched as he shrugged his shoulders.

'OK.'

It was a very different *OK* to Priscilla's, and not for the first time Eden realised Rory had been having a hard time of it lately.

'A bit fed up, huh?' Eden asked.

'I guess so.' Rory gave another apathetic shrug and let out a long sigh. When Eden didn't rush to fill the long silence, Rory finally elaborated. 'Priscilla's turned out OK now she's stopped all her whingeing.'

'And now she's going home?' Eden asked, sitting on the bed. 'Like Declan did. You miss him, don't you?'

'Even if he was just a kid, Declan was cool.'

'Declan,' Eden whispered, 'was way too cool to be five! You know,' she continued, 'that once Priscilla's gone home her bed will be filled within a few hours. Before you know it, there will be another kid in there…'

'Waking me up in the middle of the night because he doesn't know where the call bell is, or because his mum's gone home.' He gave a very weak smile. 'As soon as I've broken them in they're ready to go home.'

'You're really very good with the other patients,' Eden said. 'I know they can be a pain sometimes, but the night nurses tell me you're a real help at night if one of the other children are upset. Dianne, the night sister, told me that one night you had one of the little ones sitting on your bed at three in the morning playing a game with him when he was missing his mum and the nurses were all busy.'

A hint of a blush darkened his cheeks.

'That's really kind of you Rory.'

'I guess.' Rory was pleating the sheet and Eden noticed that his nails needed cutting, but she made a mental note rather than saying anything. She wanted to wait until Rory elaborated, finally he voiced what was really on his mind. 'School breaks up today. For Christmas,' Rory added, and Eden nodded.

'You'll be back at school by the time the summer break's over.'

'Yeah, but who will I be sitting with?' Rory growled. 'You get to meet your new teacher on the last day of term and choose who you'll be sitting beside next year. I bet I'll be sitting on my own.'

'I'll bet you're not.' Eden gave him a little nudge with her elbow. 'It might seem an age to you since I was eleven, but I can remember it very well. I can remember there was this girl in my class called Alison Davies…'

'Did you like her?' Rory asked, and Eden screwed up her nose.

'She broke her arm, just her arm, mind— nothing near as bad as you—and she was only away one week. Well, the day she came back, everyone crowded around her, wanting to sign her cast. All the teachers said that we had to be nice to *Alison.*' Eden pulled a face and managed to make Rory smile with an alarmingly good impersonation of a jealous, petulant eleven-year-old. Even her voice adopted a preadolescent surly ring. 'Everyone wanted to be *Alison Davies's* best friend.'

'Yeah?'

'Yes.' Eden grinned and corrected at the same time. 'You're going to have metal rod sticking out your legs, which is way more cool than a cast. You, Rory, are going to be fighting them off with a stick.'

'Really?'

'Really,' Eden said. 'I'm working over Christmas—well, I'm on nights for Christmas

Eve and Boxing night and then back for four nights over New Year—and I for one can't wait.'

Rory gave a very dubious frown. 'Who'd actually want to be here?'

'Me.' Eden smiled. 'Christmas is great on the children's ward.'

'For the little kids,' Rory said, but Eden shook her head.

'For everyone. I know this is probably the last place you want to be right now but, believe me, Rory, you'll remember this Christmas for ever.'

Rory gave her another dubious look. 'I doubt it. Anyway, it's not as if there's a Santa or anything.'

'Isn't there?' Eden said, treading very carefully as she spoke. Rory was at that horribly awkward age, caught between childhood and adolescence, hearing from his mates that it wasn't really true yet wanting to believe all the same. Eden thought about it for a moment and then shook her head. 'I don't care what anyone says, there's definitely magic in the air at

Christmas. You're going to have a great day, you just wait and see.'

They weren't empty words either—Christmas in hospital really was a special time and Eden felt a pang of guilt at her own selfishness, knowing the huge effort everyone went to to ensure that those who had to be there really did have a Christmas to remember. As the countdown started, the atmosphere, not just in the children's ward but around the whole hospital, heightened. A job lot of Christmas earrings must have been purchased because everywhere Eden looked the floor was being mopped or the meals were being delivered by women of all ages with twinkling Santas or snowmen dangling from their ears. The admin staff joined the party, too, with tinsel wrapped around their badges. Every ward in the hospital was decorated in its own unique way, there were massive hampers at every nurses' station, and whether you were going to borrow an ampoule of penicillin or beg for a few hospital gowns till the linen was delivered the following morning, undoubtedly a book of raffle tickets would be waved in your face—the proceeds going to raise funds for that particular ward.

Even Donna, who had insisted on good taste, stunned everyone by arriving on the ward with a stack of tabards she'd made herself for the nursing staff to wear. And when Eden arrived on Christmas Eve she was delighted to find her navy culottes and white shirt, transformed by the red tabard, covered in reindeers and jolly fat Santas that Becky handed her as she followed her into the changing room, grabbing the opportunity, while the ward was quiet, for a quick five-minute gossip before handover.

'Donna made these?' Eden checked, tying the tabard at the sides and putting in her various pens and a small torch.

'She did.' Becky grinned, sitting down on the bench and idly flicking through an ancient magazine as Eden got ready to start her shift. 'Though I'll bet she'll want them returned washed and folded by Boxing Day!'

'I am sorry,' Becky said again, for probably the hundredth time since the roster had been rearranged, looking up from her magazine and catching Eden's eyes in the mirror. 'I really feel awful that you're stuck here tonight instead of zipping up the freeway with a back seat full of presents.'

'Well, don't be.' Eden shook her head, wrapping a bit of tinsel around her ponytail. 'It's not as if I'm replacing you, Becky. You were never supposed to be working.'

'I know,' Becky sighed, 'but my house is ten minutes away. You're missing out on being with your family.'

'Becky.' Eden turned from the mirror and smiled at her friend. 'I admit I was a bit put out at first, but I soon got over it, and, as it turns out, I'm actually glad I'm working tonight. It means I'm going to spend Christmas day with—'

'Nick Watson.' Becky gave a dreamy sigh. 'You know, if I'd have known that was part of the deal when Donna asked for volunteers, I'd have put my hand straight up.'

'Becky!' Eden grinned, ignoring, for a moment the fact Becky had deliberately missed the point. Despite her smile, Eden was more than a touch concerned about the constant jaundiced air that seemed to surround Becky whenever she spoke about her marriage. 'What about Hamish?'

'What about him?' Becky rolled her eyes but her expression changed, not just her face but her entire body drooping. Her shoulders slouched, her face dropped into her hands and Eden watched as a tear slid out between Becky's fingers. Crossing the room, Eden sat down on the bench and put her arm around her friend.

'What's going on, Becky?'

'You tell me.' Becky gulped. 'He's out every night, meeting Vince or George or whatever name he can come up with.'

'People are busy around Christmas,' Eden soothed. 'Loads of parties and drinks after work.'

'Hamish doesn't have a job,' Becky pointed out, and Eden felt her heart sink. 'And even if I stretched the boundaries and gave him some grace, how come he's out every night until three in the morning?' Becky's tear-streaked face turned to Eden. 'We normally get up at six and meditate for half an hour before the kids get up, but Hamish is so worn out from the night before, I can barely raise a good morning, let alone…'

'What?' Becky frowned as Eden's hand tightened on her shoulder. Eden had nowhere to go except the honest truth.

'I love you dearly, Becky,' Eden said, her lips trying so hard not to twitch. 'And I know that none of this is funny. I just can't get past the bit about you meditating…'

'Philistine!' Becky managed a very wobbly smile. 'You should try it someday.' The tiny diversion was over and Becky took a deep breath. 'I love you too, Eden, but I hate the fact I'm sitting here on Christmas Eve pouring my heart out to you, telling you that my marriage is as good as over. He's all grumpy when I ask him where he's been, says that we've been married for ten years and that surely by now I should be able to trust him.'

'And do you?' Eden asked, but Becky just shrugged. 'He could just be…' Eden struggled to come up with a scenario, but Becky was only too happy to fill her in.

'Playing around?'

'I didn't say that.'

'You didn't have to.' Becky blew her fringe skywards. 'I know I'm not the world's tidiest wife or the best cook…' Very deliberately Eden didn't comment. 'And I know that Conner's not exactly the world's most disciplined kid, but I truly thought those sort of things didn't matter to Hamish, I really thought we were a team.'

'Talk to him,' Eden urged, and Becky nodded.

'I'm going to…'

'Just not tonight, huh?' Eden said perceptively, and Becky crumpled.

'I just want Conner to have a great Christmas. Once that's out of the way, I'm going to ask him just what the hell's going on. He's either in or out of this relationship as far as I'm concerned, not somewhere in between.'

'It will be OK,' Eden soothed, but with more conviction than she really felt. She hated the fact her friend was in so much pain, but felt powerless to help. She wished she had a little bit of the Christmas magic she'd promised Rory in her tabard to sprinkle over Becky. 'You're going to be fine, Becks.'

'I know,' Becky gulped, wiping her cheeks with her hands and standing up. 'Knowing my luck, I'll end up paying *him* spousal maintenance or, worse, he'll sell one of his stupid paintings the day I sign the divorce papers.'

'It isn't going to come to that,' Eden said, standing up as well, glancing at her watch and seeing it was just after nine. 'We'd better go into handover.'

'Thanks, Eden.' Becky sniffed. 'I feel better now.'

'I haven't done anything,' Eden pointed out.

'I was thanking you in advance.' Becky grinned. 'If I leave Hamish, Conner and I will be on your doorstep!

'Joke,' she added, linking her arm through Eden's and heading out onto the ward.

Even though the conversation had been gloomy, the mood on the ward wasn't. Every television was tuned to *Carols by Candlelight,* and the tree looking prettier somehow. The whole ward hummed with expectancy. 'Bet you can't wait for tomorrow.'

'I can't,' Eden admitted. 'I feel like a kid myself I'm so excited.' And despite what you think, it has nothing to do with Nick Watson.'

'I know,' Becky sighed. 'I was just teasing.' The conversation stopped as they reached ISO one. A tuxedo was out of place on the children's ward, especially one worn with a surgical face mask, but the tall, blond man wearing it, checking the charts outside the cubicle, carried it extremely well!

'I thought you were supposed to be at the doctors' ball,' Becky chided him.

'I'm just checking his meds,' Nick answered, ripping off the mask. 'And making sure that his day leave order is signed for tomorrow.'

'You could have rung for that,' Becky pointed out. 'And since when did you have to wear a mask to check a chart?'

'He was crying.' Nick held his hands up in a helpless gesture. 'What was I supposed to do?'

'Out, Cinderella,' Becky shooed. 'Go and have some fun. It's Christmas Eve!'

'Well, if you insist.' Nick grinned. ''Night, ladies.'

''Night, Nick,' they both answered.

'I'll pick you up around eleven?' Nick checked as he headed off, turning around, for a brief moment his eyes meeting Eden's.

'Fine.'

'Gorgeous, isn't he?' Becky sighed, but just as Eden was about to agree she realised the conversation had turned back to Ben and both women stared through the glass for an indulgent moment at the little boy sleeping on his back, his thumb half in, half out of his mouth, dark eyelashes fanning his permanently red cheeks.

'I really admire you, you know. Sometimes I feel myself getting a bit too close, getting too attached to a poor little mite that's got no one. Do you remember Dwain?'

Eden shook her head.

'He was before your time, a little guy from the Solomon Islands with leukaemia. He was just gorgeous.'

'What happened?'

'Nothing.' Becky shrugged. 'I knew I was getting in too deep so I told Donna I was getting too attached and asked not to have him allocated to me any more. And that was that.'

'But was it?'

'No.' Becky shook her head. 'Believe me, you're doing the right thing, Eden, sometimes it hurts more to walk away.'

From every room the television had the same picture, and obs were taken and meds given to the background noises of *Carols by Candlelight,* various celebrities from around Australia delivering the Christmas message through song, and on more than a few occasions Eden found herself darting into the pan room to take a steadying breath or blow her nose, only to be met by Dana or Rochelle doing exactly the same thing. The ward round on Christmas Eve on a children's ward was both the saddest and happiest place to be. Happy because who couldn't be moved by the excited chatter, the expectant faces, the palpable air of excitement as the children were tucked in for the night? But it was tempered with sadness too, sharing a pensive, brave smile with a parent who knew they had to make the most of this night, who knew, more than any parent ever should, that this Christmas was special, and that the best they could do was make the very most of this precious child that had touched their lives.

Turning off the television and quietly tying a stocking to Ben's cot, Eden gazed down.

CHAPTER SEVEN

'I'LL just take this," Eden said, retrieving the bedpan from Rory in virtual darkness, knowing how embarrassed he was by the whole procedure, 'and then I'll come and check your temperature. Merry Christmas, Rory.'

'Yeah.'

Returning two minutes later, Eden pulled out her pen torch and flashed it so she could locate his ear, pushing in the probe and listening for the almost simultaneous bleep as his temperature was recorded.

'You've got a new roommate,' Eden whispered.

'How old?'

'Twelve.' In the darkness Eden grinned as she felt Rory's interest go up a notch. 'He's feeling pretty sorry for himself. He fell off his skate-board yesterday evening and had to go to Theatre to have his arm set.'

'Was he wearing pads?' Rory whispered back, by now an expert on accident prevention.

'No.' Eden shook her head. 'I think he'll need a bit of cheering up, given it's Christmas and everything. Can I leave that to you?' She just made out Rory's nod in the darkness and even though it was six a.m., even though Rory was no doubt about to drift back to sleep, Eden was just too excited to resist. 'Why don't you have a drink?'

'I'm not thirsty,' Rory said.

'You should drink lots,' Eden insisted. 'The doctor told you that. I'll just turn on your bed-side light and pour you some water.' Flicking on the light, she fumbled with the jug and poured the reluctant Rory a drink. Seeing that he'd gone back to sleep, she pulled out her ther-mometer again, 'Sorry, Rory, I have to take your temperature again.' As Rory's eyes flicked open, Eden picked his chart off the end of his bed and started to fill it in, smothering a smile as Rory, despite the bulky traction, pulled himself to a sitting position.

'What's this?'

'What?' Eden frowned.

'This,' Rory said, gesturing to the massive bedspread covering him, with just his foot, hanging from the traction, sticking out the end of the bed. 'What's all the writing?'

'I don't know.' Eden stared at the hundred or so squares that made up the bedspread. 'What is all the writing?'

'It's from school,' Rory yelped, forgetting to whisper, his face lighting up as he read all the signatures. 'From my year. There's Davey and Glen and there's Shalya…' His fingers pointed to each individual square, three weeks of lethargy disappearing as he stared at the vast expanse of messages and pictures, each one just for him. 'And that's my teacher, Mrs Park. She says it was good I was wearing my helmet…' A tiny frown puckered his brow as he momentarily looked up at Eden. 'How did this get here? Did you put it on?'

A loud squawk from the isolation rooms gave

Eden the perfect excuse to give him a very queer look. 'Me? Since when did the night staff have time to make your bed? This is from your school?'

'Yeah!' Rory stared from her to the blanket. 'If you didn't put it here, then who did?'

'I have no idea,' Eden said, but her audience was lost. Rory's attention turned back to the friends he was sure by now would have forgotten him, his Christmas already made—and it wasn't even five past six.

'Happy Christmas, Rory.' Eden smiled. Yes, he was ten years old, but he wasn't too big for a cuddle and despite her earlier protests Eden was happy she'd worked Christmas Eve as two bony arms wrapped around her neck.

'Happy Christmas, Eden, you're the coolest one here. '

'Flatterer!' Eden grinned, cuddling him back. 'But guess what? So are you!'

Six a.m. onwards was always chaotic at the best of times. Every child had their observations taken and recorded, waking babies needed to be fed, drugs and IV antibiotics had to be given—all hopefully before the arrival of the day staff at seven. But Christmas morning was, of course, even more chaotic than usual. A stocking had been placed at the end of each child's bed and each child demanded and merited more than a quick greeting on this very special day. The ward had fewer patients, due to the fact that elective surgery was cancelled over Christmas, but that also meant that the patients that were unfortunate enough to be in hospital over Christmas really needed to be there and were therefore quite poorly. That was the reason the morning round had been started fifteen minutes earlier. Blowing her fringe skywards as she glanced down at her watch, Eden wondered if she was ever going to be finished in time.

'Morning, Sister, and Merry Christmas!'

'Good morning.' Eden smiled as Donna waltzed in, immaculate as always, but instead of heading straight to her office, as was her usual practice, Donna pulled one of her handmade tabards out of her bag and proceeded to put it on.

'Where do you want me?'

'Sorry?' Eden gave her a slightly bemused look. 'It's only six-thirty.'

'It's also Christmas morning.' Donna gave a rueful smile. 'Why don't you give me that thermometer and the medicine charts and you can get on with the feeds? Young Justin is wide awake and singing for his bottle!'

'She's a good egg really,' Dana, the night nurse Eden had been on duty with, said as they met in the milk room, where Dana was making up a jug of formula and Eden was warming a bottle. 'She does this every year.'

'I don't remember her coming in last year.' Eden frowned, shaking a few drops of milk onto the back of her wrist to check it was the right temperature.

'Because she was on a late shift,' Dana explained. 'She stayed till nearly eleven on Christmas night, doing the obs and meds and letting us get on with settling a ward of thoroughly over-excited, over-fed children. Who are you feeding?' she asked.

'Justin,' Eden answered with a smile, 'which

will take about two minutes flat. He's such a little guts!'

'Well, Ben's starting to wake up. Do you want me to pop his dummy in and hopefully drag it out so that you can feed him his morning milk?'

'Please,' Eden answered, and not for the first time she was so pleased the truth was out. Far from her colleagues criticising her, they had bent over backwards to support her—this morning was a prime example. Despite his age, Ben usually drank from a training cup, but in the morning and to settle at night he still loved to have his bottle and no one was in any rush to deny Ben this small pleasure. It wasn't so much the method of feeding he loved but the contact that came with it, being taken out of his cot and cuddled in for five or ten minutes. Dana, like the rest of the team, had been only too willing to leave that pleasurable duty to Eden.

'Oh.' Eden smiled as she pushed open Justin's door and saw his mum standing there, going through Justin's stocking, smiling as she pulled out the soft teddy, rattle and little box of chocolates that Eden had placed there when she'd take Justin's two a.m. obs. 'I was just bringing him in his bottle.

'Merry Christmas,' she added, handing over the bottle. 'The chocolates are for the mums, by the way!'

'That's really kind. Merry Christmas, Eden.' A tired-looking Jenny took the bottle and picked up her angry bundle. 'And Merry Christmas to you too, little man.' Kissing her baby on the top of his head, she sat in the large chair and started to feed her son. 'The others aren't awake yet, so I thought I'd come in and give him a cuddle and then dash back to the madhouse. Justin probably won't even know the difference, but I couldn't bear to go the whole of Christmas morning without seeing him. We're all going to come up after dinner—I know it's only supposed to be two visitors—'

'That's fine,' Eden broke in. 'And I can guarantee Justin would rather it was you than me giving him his bottle. Do you want me to take a picture?'

'A picture?'

'We've got a Polaroid camera on the ward—why don't I take a photo of you both and you can take it back home?'

Finding the camera and taking the photo actually took longer than it took for Justin to drain his bottle, but Jenny was so thrilled with the result it was more than worth it.

'Here you go!' As Eden came out of Justin's room, Dana handed her Ben's bottle. 'And don't rush. Donna's like greased lightning this morning. All the meds are done and a lot of parents are here too, giving the feeds, so take your time.'

'*Den!*' Even before the door had opened, just a glimpse of his warm milk and his precious Den through the glass and Ben's tears turned off like a tap.

'Happy Christmas, Ben.' Eden smiled, and though she wanted to scoop him up for a cuddle, first she changed his nappy and then, after washing her hands, pulled open the curtains. 'Look at the sun!' Eden pointed to the bright sky, just a few tiny wisps of cloud visible that would no doubt be burnt off by the time Ben had finished his bottle. 'And what's this?' Pulling the stocking off his cot, she handed it to him, but Ben didn't know what to do with it so Eden helped him, pulling out two shiny packages that Donna had bought with wards funds and carefully wrapped.

'You soon worked that one out.' Eden laughed as Ben pulled at the shiny paper, clapping his hands in excitement at the mirror Santa had bought him. 'It ties onto your cot,' Eden explained, doing just that, marvelling at the thought Donna had put into each present because Ben was over the moon, grinning at his reflection and banging the looking-glass with his chubby hand. If Ben wasn't quite so thrilled with his next gift, Eden was—the ten dollars allocated to each child had clearly been ignored in Ben's case, because the smart navy shorts and trendy T-shirt Eden helped him to unwrap were just divine.

'You,' Eden said, finally picking him up and giving him a cuddle with his bottle, 'are going to look so handsome!'

It was actually a reluctant Eden that left the ward!

She hadn't been lying when she'd tried to cheer up Rory the previous night because, whether or not there was a Santa, there certainly was magic in the air! But it wasn't just Ben or the other children that had Eden wanting to linger just a little while longer, more the thought of seeing Nick, dressed up as Santa, but she knew that she'd regret it later—a few hours' sleep very much the order of the day if she was to have any hope of making it through lunch.

Fat chance.

She was more excited, almost, than any of the children had been last night. By the time Eden had showered and rung her family, opening the presents they had sent her and squealing over the phone in delight as she pulled out clothes, make-up and some hair straighteners, it was impossible to get to sleep. The beautiful sunny blue sky that had greeted her when she'd gone in to Ben was burning through her flimsy curtains now and, though she'd never in a million years admit it to Jim, the house was horribly quiet without the drone of his blessed music. By nine-thirty Eden had given in, choosing instead to inspect her presents rather more carefully.

Ceramic hair straighteners. Pulling them out of the box, Eden read the accompanying leaflet and looked at the before and after photos with tongue firmly in cheek. But for the hell of it she plugged them in anyway and, sure enough, it was only ten seconds or so before the red light started flickering to indicate they were ready and only another ten seconds before Eden was utterly and completely hooked! She gaped in admiration as her chocolate curls literally melted away, staring open-mouthed in wonder a mere fifteen minutes later at the sleek, dark curtain that hung around her shoulders. And now that she'd got the straight hair she'd always dreamed of, it seemed a shame to stop there. Her minimal make-up routine was transformed as she opened jar after jar of the latest mineral make-up, *buffing* the make-up into her face, *sculpting* her cheeks and *accentuating* her eyes until, Eden was positive, she could have walked down any street in New York with her very groomed head held high.

'They're divine,' Eden breathed down the phone, a second phone call most definitely merited. 'I love them.' Her voice trembled slightly. 'I love you all, too.'

'And we love you,' Lena Hadley replied. 'You're going to be OK today?'

Eden could hear the worried note in her mother's voice. 'Mum, I'm going to be fine. Look, I know it isn't the Christmas we planned but, as much as I miss being with you all, I'm going to really enjoy spending it with Ben.'

'I know,' Lena answered, and even if she didn't say it Eden could hear the inevitable 'but'.

'I'm OK, Mum. You, better than anyone, should understand that just because I'm close to Ben—'

'It's not you being with Ben that worries me,' Lena broke in, and Eden bit hard on her lip as her mother perceptively continued. 'I've given a few tots a Christmas to remember over the years and I know that the pleasure outweighs the pain, it's you spending the day with Nick that worries me.'

'We're just friends, Mum.' Eden shook her head into the phone. 'That's all we've ever been.'

'Eden?'

'OK!' Her mother's single word had Eden raking a hand through her newly straightened hair. 'Maybe I did have a crush on him when he was engaged to Teaghan, but that's been over for ages. Mum, he's dated more women in the past year than I can count and, no matter what way I look at it, I can't justify it. And I'm certainly not going to be another of his con-quests—whatever game Nick's playing to get over Teaghan, I'm not about to be a part of it!'

'Good,' Lena replied. 'But I'm just asking you to be careful today, Eden.'

'I will be,' Eden said, blushing to her roots as she peeled back the curtain, wondering how, at twenty-eight years of age and with a few hun-dred kilometres between them, her mother could still make her feel guilty when she hadn't even done anything! 'They're here—I'd better go. Merry Christmas!'"

'Merry Christmas, darling, and be careful!'

She had to be!

One look at Nick as he climbed out of his car and Eden felt her heart stick somewhere in her throat, her mother's warning merited now because, even if it was only through her window, the Nick she was witnessing away from the ward, out of the smart suit or theatre gear, was a dangerous combination indeed. Effortlessly smart, he was dressed in smart beige shorts and a black T-shirt and somehow he managed to look as smart and as groomed as he had last night in his tuxedo. The T-shirt accentuated his muscular frame and the impossible blondness of his hair. It was the first glimpse of his legs Eden had ever been privileged to see—and what a privilege. Muscular, tanned calves striding up her drive, casual leather thongs on his feet. Eden replayed her mother's warning in her head as she pulled open her door, utterly determined to feign a casual greeting, to hide the butterflies dancing in her stomach, willing herself not to fall for his undoubted charms.

Nick Watson was danger personified.

'Where's Ben?' Eden asked, peering somewhere over Nick's shoulder to the smart silver car on the nature strip.

'Merry Christmas to you, too…' Nick started, but his voice faded in mid-sentence. He was used, too used, to seeing her in uniform or casually dressed. He'd never glimpsed this side of Eden—and what a side! Those dark chocolate curls replaced with a sleek glossy curtain. Always beautiful, today she was stunning, from head to toe. Suddenly the straightforward was terribly complicated; suddenly Nick was stalling, reaching into his pocket for his sunglasses and putting them on before answering her. 'He's asleep in the car, I've left the air-conditioning on. Still, I don't want to—'

'I'm ready.' Eden practically snapped the words, utterly perturbed all of a sudden.

Even with his eyes hidden behind dark glasses she could feel the weight of his stare, every sense in her body screaming an alert, the delicious scent of him reaching her nostrils. His hair flopped forward as he bent to pick up the mountain of bags Eden had in the doorway and she had to ball her fists, dig her nails into her palms just to stop from reaching out and running her fingers through it. As Nick headed off to the car, Eden took a moment longer than was necessary to lock the front door, dragging the warm midmorning air into her lungs. Nerves caught up with her all of a sudden as she walked down the garden path, acutely aware that the powder blue linen dress her sister had sent her was maybe just a touch too short, her beaded sandals clipping on the pavers, her hand trembling slightly as she pulled open the passenger-side door.

'He's worn out.' Eden smiled, craning her neck to see Ben.

'Don't be fooled,' Nick answered. 'He's just having a power-nap—you should have seen his face when Santa came into his room. He just about pulled off my beard, he was so excited.'

'He looks great.' Eden smiled fondly, because Ben did. Out of the hospital pyjamas and dressed in *real* clothes, he looked just like any other toddler clutching a soft toy and dozing in his car-seat.

'So do you!' And there was nothing light or flip about Nick's voice, his statement delivered in a low, husky voice. Eden jerked her head to face him and even with the barrier of his shades she could feel the admiration in his gaze. 'You look stunning, Eden.'

'It won't last.' Somehow it was Eden who managed light and flip. 'My mum bought me some hair straighteners but, despite the promises, I doubt they're quite up to a warm, humid Sydney Christmas.' She was babbling—too much—wishing Nick would just tear his eyes away, wishing he would start the engine so that she could remember how to breathe again. 'Nick…' Nibbling on her thumbnail, she decided to broach one of the many things about today that had been bothering her.

'Eden?' A tiny smile twisted on his lips as he heard the nervousness in her voice.

'We haven't spoken about—I mean, we haven't worked out what we're going to say.'

'About?'

'Us!' Eden answered with a note of exasperation. 'Your parents think we're dating, so if they ask…'

'They won't.' Nick shook his head firmly. 'Just stick with the truth—we've been working together for fifteen months. We can leave the rest up to their imaginations. I'm not expecting you to start pashing me over the mince pies. Of course, if you get a sudden urge, I won't object.'

'I won't,' Eden said quickly, too quickly perhaps.

'Won't object or won't get the urge?' Nick teased. 'Look, Eden, all you have to do today is enjoy yourself. Do you think you can manage that?'

'Yes.'

'And relax, too!' Nick added, but Eden let out a rather drawn-out sigh.

'You might be pushing it there.' But now the conversation was back to the familiar friendly they did so well, now that the horrible thick tension that had suffocated her finally disappeared,

Eden managed what only a few seconds ago had seemed near impossible—finally she relaxed. Her face broke into a smile, she pulled her seat belt around her and sank back into the seat.

'Here,' Nick offered, as Eden gave the strap a few futile tugs. 'It can be a bit tricky.'

'Is there something you haven't told me, Nick?' Eden teased as he leant over and slid the belt across.

'What?' A tiny frown appeared over his glasses.

'Since when did you take to wearing blusher?' Eden laughed as he pulled off his sunglasses and checked himself in the rear-view mirror, the remnants of Santa's rosy cheeks still in place. 'Here.' She rummaged in her bag and pulled out a moisture wipe. As her hand met his cheek Eden rued the stupid mistake she'd made in an unguarded moment, the wipe dragged over his cheek, a tiny turn of his head brought him right into her personal space and even as her hand pulled away, even as she managed some idle comment about the make-up being gone now, she knew he was going to kiss her. She had anticipated the moment so acutely that when his lips met hers there was no element of surprise, no awkward jumping, just the delicious, utterly decadent feel of his mouth on hers, a kiss that had hung between them since the day they had met. Feeling his flesh beneath hers, the weight of his lips moving a delicious fraction, the scent that was so much Nick way more intimate now as she breathed him in, she relished the moment, a heady taste of his flesh, and even if it only lasted a couple of seconds, if it was practically over before it had started, it couldn't remotely have been described as friendly,

'Happy Christmas, Eden.' His eyes pierced hers, black pupils almost masking the vivid jade, his full lips darker than she remembered, hair blonder, more beautiful than she had yet acknowledged. It was like finally seeing some long revered work of art close up for the first time.

'Happy Christmas, Nick.' It was all she could manage and yet, at that moment, all she wanted for him, for herself and for Ben, too. Pulling away, she swallowed hard. 'Happy Christmas.'

The purr of the engine starting was a blessed relief, a chance to press her flaming cheeks against the cool, cool glass, her lips stinging from the brief encounter, trying and failing not to read too much into it, trying to convince herself that he didn't move her.

If Eden's tiny rented home was a mere stone's throw from the hospital, then Nick's parents' was a brief walk to choose the stone before you threw it—only the Watsons' stone definitely landed on the *right* side of the hospital! The narrow, hilly Sydney streets were easily negotiated until they came to the beach road, where the car glided through the light traffic. Eden stared out of the window at the gathered parties on the beach, some hunched around gas barbecues, some spreading blankets and emptying picnic baskets, others for the moment ignoring the food and running into the tempting Pacific Ocean. Even though she couldn't hear them, she smiled as she envisaged their excited screams as the bracing, invigorating surf met their hot bodies.

'The water looks heavenly.' Eden commented, only it wasn't idle chit-chat, just something that had to be said as you drove along the Beach Road and stared at the endlessly divine, constantly moving backdrop.

'Did you bring your bathers?' Nick asked, and Eden shook her head.

'If you want to swim I'm sure—'

'I'm not borrowing your mum's, OK?' Eden half snapped. As much as she loved the beach, as tempting as the water looked and as determined as she was to keep Nick at a very friendly arm's length, there was no way, *no way* she was heading down to the beach in some matronly bathing apparatus on loan from Nick Watson's mother.

A girl had some pride!

Flicking on the indicator and slowing down as he approached a gap in the tea-trees, a tiny sealed road Eden hadn't known existed came into view. Nick turned the car left towards the beach, when most mere mortals would have turned right, and if the view had been gorgeous before it was spectacular now. The water was so close as Eden pulled open the passenger door and stepped out, she half expected to feel it around her ankles, Nick's family home, completely stunning, was set low in the sandy rocks, the white rendered walls accentuating the blues and greens of the ocean behind. A real estate agent Eden certainly wasn't, but even a novice like her could pick out the luxurious extras—an outside shower to rinse off as you walked back along your own private beach path, the lap pool running along the side of the house. The cosy Christmas lunch Eden had envisaged for Ben seemed to be rapidly fading. The sun beat hot on her neck as she walked round to the back of the car and woke the sleepy Ben.

'Hey, Ben.' Eden smiled, picking up the docile bundle as Nick gathered not just Eden's many bags but Ben's, too.

'You two don't exactly travel light,' he grumbled, leading the way along the sandy path as

Eden, clutching Ben, completely unsure of their reception, walked shyly behind.

Her doubts vanished even before they reached the veranda—the door flung open and Christmas greetings rang out, not just to Nick but to Eden, too, and most importantly to Ben!

'Hello, Eden!' A very slender woman who looked about eighteen introduced herself as Lily, Nick's sister. 'We're all dying to meet you.' She smiled, 'Nick's told us so much about you. And you, too, Ben,' she added to Ben, whose head was tucked into Eden's shoulder, weighing up the stranger with his almond eyes. Clearly Lily passed the test because Ben suddenly lifted his head and grinned, his smile widening as they all stepped into the house.

'Eden!'

If Lily and Nick were stunning, here was the reason.

Vivian Watson was as tall and elegant as Nick yet as delicate and slender as Lily, her Nordic hair tumbling over her tanned shoulders, her smile revealing perfectly capped teeth. Any visions Eden might have had of matronly bathers were instantly dismissed—designer clothes clearly the go for Mrs Watson. Never had Eden been more grateful for her usual blast of insomnia that morning, the two hours or so she had spent getting ready worth every sleep-deprived moment! Hugh Watson was tall, but rather less groomed, with wild grey hair and rosy cheeks. He welcomed the trio into his home.

But as ravishing and sophisticated as Vivian Watson first appeared, her smile was genuine, her affectionate greeting welcoming, and as she ushered them through to the family room Eden's nerves abated—not only because of the glass of Buck's Fizz that was thrust into her hand but by the whimper of delight Ben gave at the massive Christmas tree. It was a tree that would certainly have passed Donna's request for good taste—the heavy pine branches dressed only in silver, from the star at the top to the pile of boxes at the bottom.

Wriggling to be let down, Ben stood on the polished floorboards, dancing on the spot in excitement, enchanting everyone with his eager smile. Clearly Ben was a fast learner, because he was pointing at the mountain of presents and making his way over.

'Ben.' Gently Eden pulled him back, but Vivian just laughed and took the little boy's hand, and Ben smiled up as if he'd known her for ever.

'Are you going to help me give out the presents, Ben?' Vivian asked, dropping to the floor and pulling out a very large silver box which she handed to him.

'Careful, Ben,' Eden said nervously, knowing that Ben's only reaction would be to peel away the beautifully wrapped paper. 'Give it to….' Eden waited for Vivian to step in but, clearly used to children, she just laughed, watching delightedly as a thoroughly over-excited Ben tore at the paper with gusto, drooling with delight as a shiny red fire engine was revealed. In a matter of moments the floor was littered with paper, hours of careful choosing relegated to a few moments of excited frenzy. Eden blinked at the fabulous sarong that fell out of her package, the sheerest fabric decorated in myriad colours and tiny circular mirrors around the hemline. She hoped the rather less impressive photo frame she had purchased for Nick's mother would suffice, but she beamed with delight and promptly produced a digital camera, snapping Ben, Nick and Eden gathered around a purple plastic guitar, capturing their smiling faces.

'Here.' Nick passed a slim parcel to Eden and she turned it over in her hands, trying to guess the contents, before handing Nick the present she had bought for him. She chewed her lip as he peeled off the wrapper and blushed as he gave a crow of delight.

'I've been wanting to read this!'

'It's just a book,' Eden mumbled, not sure if he was merely being polite or was actually pleased with her choice. Knowing how much Nick loved his sport, she'd bought a tennis-star-tells-all biography, and if the reviews were anything to go by, there were a few hours of reading pleasure ahead of him. Peeling open her own present, she gave a reluctant laugh as a bikini fell into her hand—thankfully not the four-triangles type but some trendy hipster shorts and a halter-neck top, exactly what she'd have chosen for herself if she'd had her credit card handy!

'You've all bought way too much.' Eden shook her head in bewilderment at the pile of presents surrounding Ben, but Vivian shooed away her protests.

'Nonsense. We're just so thrilled to have a child here for lunch. We'd have been moping around otherwise. Christmas is all about children. We all need someone to spoil on a day like this, and who is more deserving than little Ben?'

Who indeed?

Always a happy boy, today he was positively glowing. Gone for ever were the hospital pyjamas and standard-issue soap, thanks to a thoughtful gift from Nick of slippers and a dressing-gown. There was even a little electric toothbrush in a bulging toiletry bag filled with soaps, powders, creams and brushes, just like any other loved child would have had in hospital. But it wasn't the guitar or the fire engine or the clothes that had him smiling, it was being the centre of attention, being enveloped into a warm, loving family. And Eden realised that, however much Ben might or might not know, he certainly knew that this was special.

'Right.' Vivian stood up and smoothed her dress. 'I'm going to throw you all out for an hour or so, so that I can get the place ready for Christmas dinner—unless you'd like another Buck's Fizz, Eden?'

'Not for me.' Eden shook her head. 'Alcohol and night shifts aren't exactly an ideal mix.'

'Nick?' Vivian offered, waving the jug in her son's direction. 'Surely you can have one.'

'Surely not, if I'm driving,' Nick said rather tightly, and for a moment a flicker of tension crackled in the air, no doubt memories of last year bubbling to the surface. 'Once I've dropped Ben off,' he relented, giving his mum an apologetic, brief embrace.

'Here.' Without prompting, Lily appeared with a tube of sunscreen and a pair of bathers for Ben. 'We have an inexhaustible supply of kids' bathers in this house.'

'He isn't toilet-trained.' Eden hesitated, but Lily just gave a casual shrug.

'I think I've got some training bathers somewhere, I'll go and have a look. I'll get him ready for you if you like while Nick takes you over to the cottage and shows you where you're both sleeping so you can get changed.'

'Sleeping?' Eden's startled voice had Nick looking up.

'Eden's only here for lunch.' Nick grinned. 'I can only inflict you lot on her in small doses. There's a cottage in the grounds.' Nick explained to Eden. 'I generally use it when I'm sleeping over, as my mobile phone goes off at all hours. Come on, I'll show you the bathroom.'

How casually she'd said it, Eden mused as the door closed behind her. No wonder the Watsons had accepted her so easily. No doubt they were used to Nick drifting in with his latest girlfriend in tow. Peeling off her clothes, Eden thanked her lucky stars that she'd thought to shave her legs in the shower that morning.

Wearing bathers didn't particularly bother her. Most of her spare time was spent at the beach so she was nicely tanned and the stomach that peeped out between her hipsters and halter top was, if not flat, at least toned. Only her breasts caused her a moment of angst as she tied the flimsy threads at the back of her neck, hoping there would be enough support for her rather ample bosom. She stared down at the rather impressive cleavage jiggling beneath her and wished it wasn't quite so noticeable.

'Ready?' Lily looked up from rubbing cream into Ben's shoulders as Eden walked into the lounge. Despite the sarong Vivian had bought her, which was tied loosely around her waist, despite the fact she was probably more covered than the last time she'd been in this room, despite her earlier bravado about wearing bathers, as Nick looked up, she registered the bob of his Adam's apple as his eyes flicked over the length of her body. Suddenly Eden felt woefully underdressed. She could feel a blush scorching her cheeks and her nipples protruding into the Lycra fabric just at the sight of him.

Chocolate brown board shorts slung low on his hips, his stomach flat and taut as he stood up, a smattering of blond hair on his chest. There was nothing she'd have changed about Nick. Like a digital image unfolding on a computer screen, her mind processed it slowly, the golden hair darkening slightly as it met his navel, snaking down his lower stomach, a decadent sensual arrow. Eden jerked her eyes away, trying to busy herself organising Ben, but Lily had beaten her to it, finishing off applying the sunscreen and popping on his sun hat.

'An hour,' Vivian called as the foursome headed off to the beach. 'Don't be late.'

They easily could have been!

Strolling along the damp sand, feeling the waves licking their feet, Ben squealed with delight as the waves chased his little legs, the one truly endless game that the ocean always won. But Ben gave it his best shot, running away over and over again from the waves that chased him, until Nick hoisted him up on his shoulders and ploughed into the surf, waist deep in water as Lily clicked away.

'It's great to see him looking so happy.' Lily smiled, one hand shielding her eyes from the fierce midday sun, squinting as she focussed on the happy duo.

'I wasn't sure whether or not to bring him,' Eden admitted. 'I didn't know how he'd cope in a strange house, but he's having an absolute ball.'

'He is,' Lily agreed, 'but I was actually talking about Nick. It's nice to see him looking so relaxed.'

'Last Christmas can't have been good,' Eden sighed, picking up the pace as Lily started walking. 'It must have been awful for you all.'

'It was.' Lily nodded. 'But then again the Christmas before that wasn't particularly great either.' She gave a tight shrug. 'This is the first time in a long time I've seen Nick actually looking really happy, and I'm not just talking about since Teaghan died.' Picking up her long legs, she raced out into the surf to join Nick and

Ben, leaving Eden standing there, staring at the trio in the water, the jigsaw that was Nick, the jigsaw she'd spent the last year reluctantly piecing together and finally achieving a rather unsavoury fit, suddenly tossed up into the air, the pieces lying in a confused scramble now, just the same four corners that she'd started with.

Good-looking, funny, clever and—Eden realised as if for the first time, bidding a mental farewell to her newly straightened hair and racing into the surf to join them…

Terribly, terribly kind.

CHAPTER EIGHT

HUGH and Vivian hadn't wasted a single moment of that hour, because when they arrived back, dripping wet and laughing, as they opened the bi-fold doors, for a moment the causal chatter stilled. Everyone took in the magnificent table that had been laid. It groaned under the weight of its fare, the silver cloth barely visible beneath the berries and candles, the red plates and crackers. And pride of place in the middle went to a magnificent turkey, with *all* the trimmings!

'Eden loves her food.' Nick laughed as Eden let out a low groan of pleasure.

'It's not just the food,' Eden chided, 'it's everything. Oh, Vivian, it all looks wonderful.'

She wasn't just being polite. The air-conditioning had been set to arctic to battle the hot summer sun and an oven that must have been on since six a.m.—a full roast was no mean feat when the mercury was nudging forty degrees. Everyone sped off to various rooms, changing in record time, and arrived back at the dining table with hair still dripping.

'It's amazing, isn't it, Ben?' Eden smiled and placed him in the high chair, taking in the wide eyes as he surveyed the scene he was for once the centre of. She had to swallow hard for a moment and there was a dangerous sting in her eyes as she pulled a cracker with Ben. Nick helped him and held onto the stick so that Ben won,

'Happy Christmas, buddy.' Nick kissed his podgy cheek, and if ever there was a moment Eden wanted to capture it was that one.

Gone for a moment was Maxwell Benjamin Reece, a three-year-old with Down's syndrome and HIV positive, replaced instead with Ben Reece just as happy and as excited as a three-year-old should be on this special day. He discovered a passion for roasted parsnips, turned his nose up at Brussels sprouts and clapped his hands when Vivian pulled the curtains on the delectable view and Hugh brought in the flaming Christmas pudding.

'Cream or brandy butter?' Vivian waved a plate at her and Eden struggled to make a decision. 'Or bed?' Vivian grinned. 'I think you've earned it.'

'Sounds wonderful,' Eden sighed, smothering a yawn, 'but Ben's due back at the hospital at around three. I'm scared if I lie down now I won't wake up till tomorrow.'

'You're not the only one.' Nick smiled, nodding to Ben who had dozed off in his high chair, his face covered in ice cream, spoon still clutched in his hand. 'Why don't you both lie down? I'll wake you at three.'

And even though she opened her mouth to argue, not a single word of protest came out. Why shouldn't she lie down? Why should she rush Ben back to the hospital when he still had a precious hour?

'You won't think I'm horribly rude?' Eden

checked, but the entire Watson clan just rolled their eyes and shooed her away.

'I'll take you over to the cottage,' Nick said, but when Eden frowned he softened it with a smile. 'You won't get any sleep in the house. Mum's on her third sherry *and* she's just discovered the karaoke machine!'

They walked through the garden in amicable silence, Nick carrying a sleeping Ben. Eden struggled just to keep her eyes open and barely took in her surroundings as Nick gave her a very brief tour of the essentials, pointing out the phone, kitchen and bathroom before pushing open a bedroom door. Never had a bed looked more tempting!

'You'll come and wake me?' Eden said.

'Yes. Have a good sleep.' Nick closed the door.

Eden didn't need to be told twice. Not even bothering to pull back the sheets, she just laid Ben down on the pillow before gratefully stretching her exhausted, utterly full body out on the bed, smiling as Ben cuddled in to her.

'You're not that hard to get to sleep really, are you?' Eden whispered. 'You just want someone with you.'

A deep voice summoned her. Nick's face swam briefly into focus as she struggled to open her eyes.

'It's three o'clock. We ought to be getting Ben back.'

'Mmm.' Sleepily she agreed and struggled to sit up, but as Nick pushed her back down onto the pillow she didn't resist.

'I'll take him back. You have a sleep, you're exhausted.'

'I'll be OK.' Eden shook her head. 'Just give me five minutes.'

'Go to sleep,' Nick whispered, and it sounded so easy, so completely straightforward she was tempted to comply.

'Give Eden a kiss, Ben, and she'll see you tomorrow.'

'Den!'

His perpetually wet lips splashed onto her cheek and she held him close for a fierce second.

'Den and Ben.' Even though her eyes were closed she could hear Nick's smile as he said the words and lifted Ben up off the bed. 'Come on, buddy, let's get you back.'

Opening her eyes in the darkened room, Eden took a moment or two to orientate herself. Fumbling for her watch, she was bemused to see that it was after six, stunned to realise it was Christmas Day and absolutely horrified to find that Ben wasn't lying beside her.

'He's fine.' The door was pushed open and Nick smiled as he made his way over. 'You were completely out for the count so I took him back to the hospital myself.'

'How was he?' Eden asked, sitting up and trying to give the impression she was, if not entirely together, at least awake!

'Great,' Nick said, his smile widening as he sat on the bed beside her. 'He was just great, Eden, he had the best day. I've never seen a kid so happy and so tired at the same time. Mum printed off a couple of the pictures on the camera and he's lying in his cot back on the ward in his new pyjamas surrounded by his new toys, with his new CD playing and a photo of us all in his hand.'

'I didn't say goodbye,' Eden started, but Nick shook his head.

'You did. You just can't remember it. He gave you a kiss.

'How about some supper?' Nick asked, changing the subject and standing up. 'My sisters' kids are here now and mum's put out a cold buffet.'

'I should get back,' Eden said, but Nick wouldn't hear of it.

'For what, Eden? You can't be on your own on Christmas night.'

'Why not?' Eden shrugged. 'Anyway, once you've given me a lift, you can relax and have a drink, enjoy Christmas night with your family.'

'Stay,' Nick said. 'Stay here the night.'

'With you?' Eden said startled. 'I think that's pushing the deal a bit, don't you?'

'I can sleep on the sofa, or if you'd rather I didn't stay here, I could ask Mum to make up the bed in the spare room over at the house,' Nick offered.

'And ruin your little charade. Oh, come on, Nick, I'm sure you can manage to behave yourself for one night.' She gave a tiny tight smile, a slight edge to her voice, which she quickly modified. 'After all, we both know we're just good friends. It's no big deal.'

But it was.

Even as Eden agreed, even as she casually shrugged and nodded, she could sense the folly of her decision, hear her mother's warning words ringing in her ears. Sure, at the moment the talk was flowing easily and they were the friends that they supposedly always had been, but as she wandered up to the main house and through to the lounge, saying hi to Lily's kids and helping herself to the gourmet buffet, she could feel Nick's eyes on her, feel the strong current of emotion beneath the apparent calm surface, knew deep down inside that things weren't all they seemed—however brief the kiss, something had happened in the car. A point of no return had been passed and tonight things would come to a head.

Tonight, she would find out where she stood.

Lily's children had clearly inherited more than a few Watson genes! Fair and good looking, they were all thoroughly spoiled and had a rather haughty arrogance that Eden assumed was hereditary when you were born with wealth, brains and beauty.

'Are you Uncle Nick's new girlfriend?' Aqua green eyes, identical to her uncle's, narrowed as they eyed Eden. Nick's precocious niece, Harriet, stared rudely at Eden as she shuffled her food around her plate.

'I am,' Eden replied carefully, consoling herself that it was more a lie by omission. After all, she was a girl and, as Nick had pointed out on rather too many occasions, she was also a friend.

'Are you two going to get married?'

'Harriet!' Lily chided as Eden took refuge in her turkey sandwich. 'Don't be so personal!'

'Well,' Harriet sniffed, 'I heard Nanny say

Eden was staying the night in Uncle Nick's room, so I certainly *hope* that they're getting married.'

Fortunately Eden had a mouthful of turkey at the time and was saved from comment, but she was sorely tempted to poke her tongue out at the impossibly bold child and privately wished Lily would put them all to bed. But, as the evening progressed, when it became clear the little treasures were going to be up longer than the adults, Eden finally gave in and relaxed. The plates were cleared away and the corny party games that were so much a part of Christmas unfolded, and Eden found herself joining in. Finally, when she was exhausted, she flopped on the sofa and the yawn she was smothering was interrupted as she laughed out loud as Harriet took to the karaoke machine, belting out a song. Her brothers joined in and, turning, Eden was slightly startled to see a sparkle of tears in Lily's green eyes.

'They're having such a good time,' Lily sniffed. 'I've been so worried about Christmas, wondering how they'd cope, what with their dad and I breaking up and everything—we parted in April,' Lilly added.

'I'm sorry,' Eden responded, feeling horribly out of her depth, wondering just how much, as Nick's *girlfriend,* she should know. 'It must have been a difficult time for you all.'

'It was.' Lily nodded. 'I was running around trying to help Nick. Well, you'd know yourself the state he was in, riddled with guilt, barely sleeping, a complete mess really…'

Lily was too deep in her own thoughts to register Eden's frown. By April Nick had appeared well over Teaghan, in fact, if she remembered correctly, by April Nick had been well on his way to his second girlfriend and coping remarkably well, nothing like the shattered man Lily was portraying.

'I was so busy trying to be there for Nick I didn't realise until it was too late that my own life was falling apart.' This time she did notice Eden's frown. 'Another woman,' Lily explained, with more than a dash of bitterness. 'There I was, feeling sorry for him working so hard, and all the time…' She let out a low mirthless laugh. 'I'm sorry, you don't need to hear all this. I'm just finding it hard to keep the smile painted on at the moment. This time last year I thought I knew where I was going, had this vision of the future, and it didn't include being a single mother.'

'Don't be sorry,' Eden said. 'My friend's going through the same thing at the moment, or at least she thinks she is. She's just hoping to make it through today without upsetting the kids so that they can have a good Christmas, and then she's going to confront him.'

'The things we do for our kids,' Lily said softly, looking over to her brood dancing and laughing as if they didn't have a care in the world. They waved back to their mum who grinned and waved back. Eden could only admire her, just as she had admired Priscilla's mum, women who somehow held it together, somehow kept things going, somehow managed to keep on keeping on, despite being on their own.

The rather sombre mood on the sofa was lifted when Nick finally wrestled the microphone from Harriet, and both women laughed as he showed that he really was the biggest kid in the room, singing loudly, his face one of pure concentration as he tried to follow the little ball over the lyrics on the TV screen as the kids all fell about laughing.

'He can sing, too,' Eden said dryly.

'Yep.' Lily laughed. 'There's nothing my brother can't do if he sets his mind to it. You know, I'm really glad that you two finally got it together.'

Oh, how Eden would have loved to have probed further, how she wanted to ask just what Lily meant. Instead, she had to make do with sipping her drink, grateful for the diversion when Vivian stood up and clapped her hands. 'How about a game of charades?'

'How about we call it a night?' Nick said, coming over and smiling down at Eden who was clearly having trouble keeping her eyes open. A few hours' sleep in the afternoon not quite enough to keep her partying into the small hours.

'You stay,' Eden offered, but Nick shook his head.

'I'm tired, too. I've been up since six.'

The goodnights took for ever and for Eden they were surprisingly hard. The family she had shared Christmas Day with had already wormed their way into her heart and she was achingly aware that it wasn't just goodnight she was saying but probably goodbye, too, that the game of charades had started long, long ago and that her allotted time slot in Nick's vibrant life was nearly over.

'They're great.' Eden smiled when finally they were at the cottage. She felt impossibly shy now, the exhaustion that had sedated her moments ago disappearing, nerves catching up as she faced Nick alone for the first time that day. 'They've all been so nice. I feel absolutely wretched that we've deceived them.'

'What they don't know can't hurt them.' Nick shrugged, pulling a pillow off the bed. 'I'll crash on the sofa.'

'Nick.' Eden gave a dry laugh. 'It's only about

two feet long and there aren't exactly a load of spare sheets. Just sleep in the bed.'

'You're sure?'

'So long as you don't snore.' Eden grinned. 'Not that it would matter—I'm so tired I'll be out like a light in a couple of minutes anyway.'

In record time Eden peeled down to her knickers and bra, jumped into the bed and pulled the sheet around her, pretending not to watch as Nick pulled off his shorts and T-shirt, stripping down to his boxers. She was as rigid as a board as Nick slowly climbed into his side of the bed, and as she felt the indentation of the mattress beside her she desperately tried to keep her breathing even as Nick flicked off the light. Not that it made much difference. The full moon over the bay cast a silver glow around the room. 'I've had a fabulous day.'

'So have I,' Nick agreed. 'In fact, it's been the best Christmas I can remember in a long time, and it's thanks to you, Eden.'

'To me?'

She felt him roll over to face her, but still she lay staring at the ceiling, terrified to face him, terrified he might somehow read the blatant desire in her eyes. 'You've made this Christmas really special.'

She didn't know what he meant—whether he was referring to Ben or that he had been saved a few awkward questions from his parents. But his face was right beside her now and she was powerless not to look at him. Her head turned on the pillow and she swallowed hard as she finally faced him, the eyes that had held hers in the car staring down at her. All she could do was gaze back, gaze back at the man she had always, since the moment she'd set eyes on him, loved. Knew there and then that, however much she fought it, however much she didn't understand it, she loved him and probably always would.

'I hate going to bed on Christmas night.' Her voice trembled slightly. 'Hate knowing that Christmas is over.'

'It doesn't have to be,' Nick whispered, and Eden knew exactly what he meant.

For a moment the voice of reason sounded loudly in her mind, her eyes taking in the effortlessly beautiful man that lay before her, a man who had broken more hearts in this last year than she cared to remember, a man who would undoubtedly do the same to her. But need was taking over, tossing aside reason, soothing her with impossible truths—that surely she could deal with this, that one night with Nick was enough to see her through, that because she knew what she was getting into, maybe it wouldn't hurt too much…

'I've always wanted you, Eden.' Nick's voice was thick with emotion, his finger tracing the contour of her cheek, and she screwed her eyes tightly closed, trying to summon up the mental strength to push away what she wanted so dearly. 'I've always wanted you.'

His repetition was enough to convince her, enough to drown out the warning bells, and Eden knew, as she had known since she'd agreed to stay the night, that this moment had been sure to arrive, the thrum of sexual tension that had hung in the air between them demanded this natural conclusion. And more selfishly perhaps, as wonderful a day as she'd had, as much pleasure as there was in giving as well as receiving, Eden wanted her own Christmas magic now, wanted to peel away the wrappers on the one present she'd secretly wished for for so long now, wanted to feel him, to touch him, to be held by him, to know him as only a lover could.

Her eyes stared into the endless depths of his. No need for barriers now, the desire, the passion she felt was there for him to see. He read her so well, his beautiful face swimming out of focus as he softly lowered his lips to hers, the sweet, sweet release of his mouth on hers, the cool of his tongue languorously exploring her mouth a delicious backdrop as their bodies met.

He turned her to face him and she felt his naked skin against hers, the brush of his thigh, the quiet strength of his arm around hers. And all she could do was kiss him back. She relished the feel of his skilful hand on her, expertly undoing her bra. His hand cupped the swollen weight of her full breast, his mouth leaving hers now and exploring the hollows of her throat. Eden revelled in it—his expert touch, the sheer intimacy of sharing a bed, sharing each other.

What she lacked in skill she made up for in willingness. There wasn't a more decadent scent in the world than that of a man in full arousal and she dragged it in, drew on its aphrodisiac power, Nick's sheer naked delight in her body imbuing her with boldness. She ran a tentative finger along the snaking trail of his abdomen that had teased her earlier, fumbling with the elastic of his boxers and sliding them down over his snake-like hips. As Nick wriggled out of their confines she laid eyes on his naked body for the first time.

Eden stumbled into her own paradise, capturing the full delicious length of him in her hand, marvelling at the silky texture, the ominous strength, running a curious, needy, teasing finger in ever-decreasing circles.

'Careful.' Nick's gasp was deep, his breathing rapid, and if ever Eden had felt empowered it was then. For a moment in time at least she held Nick Watson in the palm of her hand, and it was she, Eden, calling the shots.

'Why?'

The innocence of her question belied the wanton smile on her lips, her fingers working intimate magic, feeling the delicious swell of him beneath her touch as Nick's breathing came harder. In the moonlight she could see the planes of his stomach, the golden dust of hair, the generous length of him rising, the pleasure to be had in giving clearer now because Eden's breath was coming faster. His fingers dug into her breasts as his other hand cupped one buttock and it was Nick taking control now, Nick guiding her down onto him, Nick parting the petals of her most intimate place, Nick gazing up at her, holding her steady as she slid down his glorious length.

Capturing the peach of her buttocks, he guided her towards oblivion, that distant beat nearing now, Nick so deep inside her body, inside her head that for a second she resisted the deliciousness, not wanting to give in, not wanting it to be that easy, not wanting it all to be over, feeling the final, thrusting swell of him, the tension in his body beneath her, until Eden gave into her own blessed release, reeling at the force of her orgasm, almost violent in its intensity, robbing her of any semblance of control. Her neck arched back as she dragged him in deeper, a rush of heat fanning her throat, scalding up her spine, making her giddy with sated lust, heady from spent emotions, the last embers of her fire dying down, until spent, utterly exhausted, she lowered her head to his chest, listened to his heart pounding in her ear, the sheen of his damp chest on her cheek mingling with an involuntary tear that slipped out of one eye.

'Hey.' Nick rolled her on her side, wiping the salty tear away with the nub of his thumb.

'I'm fine,' Eden whispered. 'I'm just…' But she didn't finish, couldn't even attempt to find the words to describe how she felt at that moment, lying in bed with Nick's strong arms around her, her body weak, exhausted but supremely satisfied, the breeze of the ceiling fan cooling her warm flesh, a glimpse of a perfection she had always known existed, a feeling of coming home.

'Happy Christmas, Eden,' Nick whispered, kissing the top of her head, dragging her just a fraction closer towards him.

She nodded into the darkness even though his words didn't require a response because, quite simply it was the happiest Christmas she'd known.

CHAPTER NINE

THE shrill ringing of Nick's mobile phone had Eden sitting up before her eyes had even opened. She wrapped the sheet around her and blinked as Nick jumped out of bed and pulled on his boxers, clearly, due to his profession, used to being abruptly woken. Raking his blond hair into almost perfect shape, he headed out into the hall with a very brief 'I won't be long'.

Without even looking at her watch, Eden knew they had both overslept. Bright sunlight streamed through the windows, emphasising the chaos of the discarded clothes and rumpled bed, her naked body beneath the sheet swift confirmation, if Eden had needed it, of what had taken place last night. But instead of reeling in horror, instead of burning with shame and burying her head beneath the sheet, Eden gave a contented sigh and lay back on the pillow, staring at the ceiling and fondly recalling their love-making, remembering the bliss of being held by him, the tenderness in his eyes and, best of all, the depth of his words.

He'd always wanted her.

As he walked back into the bedroom, utterly confident, completely without regret, Eden turned to face him, smiling as he placed a brimming cup of coffee on the bedside table. She took a grateful sip.

'I thought you could use a coffee.' Nick gave a very tight smile and Eden frowned at the stilted voice. 'And then I'm going to have to take you home, I just had a phone call…' He didn't elaborate further, just gave a shrug of his shoulders. 'If you need a couple of paracetamol or anything, I can get them for you.'

'Sorry?' Bewildered, she frowned at him, trying to catch his eye and realising he was avoiding her gaze, the implication behind his offer starting to sink in. 'Nick, I barely had anything to drink last night. I certainly don't have a hangover.'

'I was just offering.' Nick gave another tight shrug and Eden stared at him, perplexed. All she knew was that she had to tell him her truth, couldn't let him think for even a moment that last night was something she regretted, that she could be so easy as to tumble into bed and make love with a man on nothing more than a whim.

'Nick.' Her hand reached out to touch him, capturing his forearm in her fingers, holding it as she spoke, trying somehow to recapture the closeness that had so recently been there. 'I don't regret last night for a moment. Last night wasn't something that happened just because I was feeling tired or emotional or because I'd had a few too many to drink. Last night was because of how I feel about you, how I've *always* felt about you.'

'No!' Shaking his head, he shrugged off her hand, his voice when it came harsh and unfamiliar an utter contrast to the man that had softly held her only a matter of hours ago.

'Eden, we're friends, that's all we've ever been. Last night was just….'

'Just what, Nick?' Eden croaked, eyes wide in her pale face, reeling from the mental slap to her cheek he had just delivered.

'One of those things,' Nick answered, his voice ominously flip. 'Two friends getting a bit emotional, perhaps.'

'Nick.' Eden was struggling to keep her voice down, struggling to fathom the change in him, refusing to believe that things could change so quickly, that he could use her so readily, could toss her aside so easily. 'Last night you said that you'd always wanted me, last night—'

'I didn't.'

His denial floored her, his absolute refusal to admit the truth so incredible that all she could do was stare at him, her mouth open but no words coming out, shame burning onto shame, a dark blush of humiliation spreading over her cheeks.

'I didn't say that, Eden,' Nick insisted, as he looked her straight in the eye and swore that black was white. 'You're getting things mixed up.'

'Oh, I'm mixed up all right!' Eden retorted. 'I'd have to be, to be stupid enough to get into bed with you.'

'Eden.' His voice was incredibly calm, as if it were she, Eden, who was the one with the problem, his barefaced lies, his outright denial, his complete about-turn clearly par for the course for Nick. 'I'm sorry you're feeling this way—'

'No, you're not,' Eden interrupted, her face incredulous as she stared back at this stranger. 'And don't presume to know how I'm feeling, Nick, don't presume a single thing about me ever again.' Draping the sheet around her, Eden stood, and if awkwardness about her breasts had taught her one thing, it was how to pull on a bra and knickers while still covered, those awkward adolescent days at the swimming pool finally coming in useful for something! 'Is that the line you use to get women into bed, then? Make out it actually means something to you, tell whoever it is that you're shagging that night that you've always felt something for them?'

Her words hit their mark. Nick winced at her unfamiliar crudeness, but he didn't back down and for Eden it was the final straw. She hated herself for it, hated the shame that had assailed her, last night sullied now for ever. But if she hated how she felt, at that moment she hated Nick more, and it gave her the strength to continue, to tell him in harsh, whispered tones exactly what she thought of him. Eden was grateful for that moment, glad of a chance to vent her anger, to say what was on her mind before remorse took over, knowing that the next time she faced him it would be she, Eden, looking away.

'You're a user, Nick Watson. I don't know what your problem is, whether you're trying to sleep your way out of your own grief or, worse, you've just forgotten how to care any more.

'Well, don't worry, Nick, I won't be hanging around and making a nuisance of myself. I won't be coming up to you in pubs and trying to buy you a drink, like Tanya was, in some pathetic hope that we can take a trip down memory lane…'

A muscle was leaping in his cheek, but apart from that he was completely motionless.

Emotionless

'You used her, Nick, the same way you used me,' Eden said, confused, bewildered but completely in control. Not bothering to ask permission, she picked up a comb from his dresser and ran it through her hair before slipping on her sandals. 'Now, can you, please, take me home?'

Because they were nice, decent people who didn't deserve their Christmas to be spoilt, Eden managed a friendly smile and a few polite exchanges as she said farewell to Nick's family, but tears were dangerously close as she walked out to Nick's car. Despite her casual wave as Nick pulled out of the driveway, her whole body was trembling inside, scarcely able to fathom that things could have gone so horribly wrong, that she could have misread him so badly, that the man she loved could treat her like this.

Had loved.

A tiny spark of hope flared inside her as Eden mentally corrected herself—a woman's survival instinct kicking in, the knowledge that she would get through this, that she would come out the other side. And that knowledge gave her the strength to turn to him as he pulled up outside her house, to look him in the eye and keep her voice even as she spoke.

'I'd appreciate it if you didn't tell anyone what happened last night.'

'What do you take me for?" Nick responded, clearly irritated by her request. 'You know I wouldn't say anything.'

'But I don't know you,' Eden pointed out, as his eyes refused to meet hers and he turned his face away. 'I'm looking at you, Nick, and I don't even know you, but I'm telling you this much—I'll smile and I'll be friendly and I'll be completely professional, but don't be fooled, don't for one minute think that I've forgotten what a sleaze you really are. Don't ever, even for a second, think that I've forgiven you.'

Opening the car door, she swung her legs to the pavement outside and stood up, frowning as Nick called her back.

'What?'

'You forgot these.' He still wasn't even looking at her, just staring fixedly at the street ahead as one hand held up the bag with the presents she had acquired yesterday. But in a small defiant gesture Eden declined, instead slamming the car door closed and heading up the drive. She pulled out her keys and, despite her shaking hands, slid the key easily into the lock, opening the door and stepping inside. With the door safely closed behind her she stared at the blinking light on the answering machine, knowing it would be her mother checking that everything was OK, that Eden had heeded the warnings and kept her head.

And only when she heard the purr of his engine, only when she knew that he was really gone, that Nick wasn't coming back, did she let out a strangled sob and finally give in to the tears that had been there since he'd walked back into the bedroom that morning, since he'd offered her a coffee as he'd cruelly ripped out her heart.

CHAPTER TEN

'CAN you believe that all that time he was working at the post office?'

A delighted Becky tucked in the end of the sheet at the bottom of Rory's bed as Eden did the same on the other side, sliding it up under Rory, as he held onto his monkey bar, and tucking it in at the top.

'There was me thinking…well, you know, and all the time he was saving up to buy me these!' Fondly she touched the diamond studs in her ears and Eden gave her patient a small eye roll, smiling as Rory gave one back.

For the most part, this type of conversation took place away from the bedside, but Rory, beyond bored with the hospital routine, delighted in being included in the nurses' more private conversations and loved being made to feel special.

'Aren't they lovely?' Becky said for the hundredth time. 'You should have seen my face when I opened the parcel.'

'They're gorgeous,' Eden agreed. 'Aren't they, Rory?'

'Yep.' Rory nodded, winking at Eden as he spoke. 'You look great in them, Becky!'

The bed changed, Eden and Becky carefully tucked in Rory's beloved blanket. Since Christmas morning, when he'd received his gift, Rory had been a different boy indeed, the despondent gloom that had shrouded him gone now. He felt safe in the knowledge that he hadn't been forgotten by his peers.

'Are you two both on night shift, then?' Rory checked, and Eden nodded.

'You've got us for the next four nights, so you'd better behave.'

'How come you have to do so many nights, Eden?' Rory asked innocently, completely unaware of the battles that went on behind making up the nursing roster.

'It's just the way my shifts fall,' Eden said casually, smiling as Donna came over to say she was leaving. Her jacket was on and her bag firmly on her shoulder, ready to call it a night after a long late shift.

'But that will mean you have to work Christmas Eve and New Year's Eve,' Rory said loudly, completely unabashed by Donna's presence, blissfully unaware of the politics of hierarchy. 'It doesn't seem fair that you have to work both.'

'It's no big deal,' Eden said, smothering a smile as Becky gave a delighted grin behind Donna's stern face, both women scarcely able to believe their luck that Donna had heard what Rory had just pointed out!

'Could I have a quick word, you two?'

They headed off to the nurses' station, no doubt, Eden thought, to be told that if they got a quiet few moment there were several hundred cupboards that needed cleaning or a mountain of stores to be put away. But Donna had other things on her mind. 'I've just had a call from Emergency and we're getting a new admission—a five-year-old presenting with her first seizure. She's mildly febrile but, given her age, the emergency staff don't think it was a febrile convulsion. I've allocated ISO 2 for her until we know what's going on.'

Eden jotted the information down on her pad, slightly surprised at the seriousness of Donna's voice and the fact she had pulled both staff members away to tell them about the new admission. PUO, or pyrexia of unknown origin, and a first seizure were both fairly routine, but as Donna continued talking Eden's pen stilled over the paper and, unlike Becky, realised in an instant why they had been called aside.

'Her name's Harriet Mason.'

'Martin?' Becky asked.

'No, Mason,' Donna reiterated. 'You both need to know that this patient is Nick Watson's niece—he's down in Emergency with her now, but even though it's Dr Watson on take tonight, young Harriet has been admitted under the care of Dr Timms so if there are any problems in the night, instead of consulting one of Nick's team, you'll need to ask switch to page one of Dr

Timms's team, though naturally, if it's an emergency or she starts seizing, it will just have to be the doctor nearest who treats her. Hopefully it won't be Nick.'

'Hopefully,' Eden agreed. 'How long till Emergency sends her up?'

'I told them to bring her when they're ready. I shouldn't think they'll be very long.'

With that in mind Eden and Becky headed off to set up the room, turning back the bed and putting out a gown and kidney dish in case Harriet felt sick, checking that the oxygen and suction were all connected and in proper working order.

'Do you want to take her?' Eden offered rather too lightly, colouring up a touch as Becky gave her a rather quizzical frown, no doubt puzzled. On night shift it was generally a case of whoever saw the patient first was the one who admitted them, but the last thing Eden needed right now was a close encounter with Nick. It had been hard enough maintaining an air of professionalism the few times their paths had crossed over the last few nights, but the fact his niece was a patient and that Eden knew Lily could only make things difficult.

'Sure,' Becky replied. 'Eden, is everything OK?'

'Everything's fine.' Eden replied stiffly, needlessly rechecking the wall-mounted suction again.

'You never really said how your Christmas went,' Becky pushed. 'What it was like at Nick's.'

'I had a great day,' Eden answered, forcing a smile and turning around. 'Ben did, too. Nick's family made us both very welcome.'

The sound of the ward doors opening thankfully ended the difficult conversation, and Eden peered out of the window. 'Your patient's here, Becky. I'll go and do the meds and then I'll give Rochelle a hand with the obs and settling.'

'Save some work for me,' Becky called, waving to the shadowy figure of the porter pushing the gurney along the darkened ward as Eden dashed off and set about her work. But as much as she feigned indifference, it wasn't only Nick's presence that was upsetting her. The fact

Harriet had been taken sick so suddenly had a knot of anxiety tightening in Eden's stomach, coupled with a surge of sympathy for Lily, who had already been through so much this past year, and a genuine hope that Harriet would be OK.

'How's Harriet?' Eden asked a short while later when Becky came to help with the night round, catching up at the nurses' station and checking the IV antibiotics.

'Good,' Becky replied. 'She's on two-hourly neuro obs, her temp's 37.8 and she seems comfortable with it. Her mum's staying the night.' Becky shot her a sideways look. 'She was asking after you. She said you had a great time on Christmas *night!*' Swallowing hard, Eden deliberately ignored Becky's not too subtle push for information but, not remotely fazed, Becky carried on fishing. 'I thought you were only there for a few hours at lunchtime.'

'I stayed for supper,' Eden said lightly, tapping a bubble out of a syringe.

'And breakfast, too?' Becky giggled but it

faded midway, seeing the anguished look on Eden's face. 'Oh, Eden, I didn't mean to…' Helplessly she flailed, 'Eden, I had no idea—'

'Leave it, Becky,' Eden's voice came out more sharply than she'd intended, but a ride on the rumour mill was the very last thing she needed right now. 'I mean it, if you breathe a single word to anyone…'

'As if I would,' Becky soothed, concern growing in her kind eyes as Eden rapidly blinked back a threatening tear. 'Eden, what on earth happened?'

'I can't talk about it.' Eden shook her head, taking a tissue from a box and blowing her nose, but Becky was insistent.

'But it might help,' Becky said. 'Look at all my troubles with Hamish. You were there for me, Eden, and you know I'd never breathe a word. And who knows? It might even help.'

'It won't,' Eden said firmly.

'It might.' Instinctively Becky's hand reached for her earlobe, fingering one of the precious jewels Hamish had bought for her, and Eden managed a weak smile.

'Believe me, Becky, there's going to be no little box with a bow for me. I know you'd never breathe a word, I trust you implicitly. It's just that I insisted that Nick not say anything to anyone. It's only fair that I do the same.'

'Fair enough.' Becky nodded 'But if you change your mind, you know that I'm here for you.'

'Thanks,' Eden sniffed. 'Now, let's get on with checking these drugs or we're never going to finish. Poor Rochelle's done practically all the obs herself.'

'She's good, though,' Becky observed. 'Considering she's just a grad nurse, she's incredibly efficient.'

'How's Harriet?'

The sound of Nick's voice behind them had both women jumping, and never had Eden been more grateful that the conversation had shifted to Rochelle. The last thing she needed was for Nick to see how upset she was. Thankfully, Becky had it all under control, turning her smiling face to Nick and somehow managing to greet him in the same easygoing way that she always did.

'She's doing great, Nick,' Becky answered, as Eden busied herself with the IV drugs, laying out the open prescription charts and placing the kidney dishes with the checked medication on top, then attaching a little sticky note to each kidney dish with the schedule time clearly visible. Impeccably organised, especially where medication was concerned, Eden was glad of the distraction, glad to be able to busy herself as Nick and Beck chatted on. 'Her obs are still stable, just a little bit febrile—37.8 I've given her a drink of milk and she's settling to sleep.'

'And Lily?' Nick checked. 'My sister?'

'Like any other mum, worried out of her mind and trying not to show it. Harriet's in ISO 2.'

'Thanks.' Nick nodded, but didn't head off. Instead, he tapped Harriet's details into the computer and checked to see whether or not any labs were back on her. 'You know that she's due for an EEG in the morning?'

'All booked.' Becky smiled. 'Any blood results back yet?'

'Just her U and Es,' Nick replied, 'which are all normal. Emergency's really busy, so I think Harriet's bloods will take a while to come back. Can you let me know when they do?'

'Sure,' Becky answered, looking up as Eden came over.

'Ready to give the IVs?' Eden asked, then, smiling casually, she greeted Nick. 'Hi, Nick, I'm sorry to hear about your niece.'

'Thanks.' Nick forced a smile of his own. 'I'd better go and say goodnight to her and then I'll be in my office tonight. Call me if there's any change.'

'We will,' Eden assured him.

As he marched off Becky let out a tiny gasp of admiration. 'Wow, you're good. Talk about laid-back. How on earth did you manage it?'

Eden gave a mirthless laugh. 'A full year of practice, Becky.'

* * *

The round took for ever and by the time the charts were all filled in and ruled off for the next day, it was already half past two.

'Do you want to go for your supper break?' Becky offered Eden as a tired-looking Rochelle returned from hers.

'You go,' Eden answered. 'Cot three's due to wake any moment. I'm just warming a bottle for him in anticipation.'

Becky stood up gratefully, smothering a yawn as she did so. 'I won't say no. I'm exhausted. I'll just stretch out in the staffroom. If I'm not back on time, come and call me.'

'Will do,' Eden answered, after all her years in nursing still baffled how anyone could manage to sleep on their break and come back to work afterwards saying that they felt better for it. Eden had tried it once and had sworn never to do it again, preferring to use her break to flick through a few magazines or read a book. 'Is there anything that needs doing while you're gone?'

Becky shook her head. 'I'm up to date. Just some oxygen sats to be done on cot one at three a.m.' Her face suddenly dropped. 'Oh, and Harriet will need another set of neuro obs at three. I can stay if you like and go after—'

'I'll be fine,' Eden assured her, consoling herself that Lily would no doubt be asleep. She was determined not to let her personal life interfere with her work. 'You go. Enjoy your break.'

As Eden had predicted, Justin awoke a couple of minutes later and because she was the most senior RN on the ward Eden put on a gown and bought him to the desk, cuddling him as she gave him his bottle.

'He's been here for ages,' Rochelle said, peering at her notes. 'Why has he been kept in so long? There doesn't seem to be anything wrong with him.'

'It's complicated,' Eden replied warily, smiling down at the baby as he guzzled his bottle. 'Justin was bought in a few weeks ago with failure to thrive. He was losing weight and not taking his feeds well.'

'Well, that's certainly improved.'

'That's exactly the problem,' Eden responded. 'He put on weight and was discharged, only to present to his GP a couple of weeks later with further weight loss. He's been in all this time having tests to see what the problem could be.'

'But they've all come back as normal,' Rochelle said, staring down at her notes. 'Clearly he's taking his feeds well now, so why don't they just send him home?'

'Here's perhaps not the best place to talk about it,' Eden said tactfully, 'but when Becky gets back from her break, if we get a chance we can go into the office.'

'Oh.' Rochelle's eyes widened, staring from Eden to Justin and shaking her head. 'But his mum adores him,' Rochelle said.

'We'll talk later,' Eden said again, because the nurses' station, even if it was in the middle of the night, wasn't the place to discuss such things.

Jenny did love Justin, there wasn't any doubt on that score, but for so far inexplicable reasons whenever the child had been left in her care, he had not only failed to thrive but had actually lost weight and was suffering from malnutrition to the point where he had rickets from a vitamin D deficiency. After exhaustive investigations the medical and social workers were coming to the unpalatable conclusion that young Justin might be a victim of a rare and controversial syndrome by the name of Munchausen's by proxy—that his mother was somehow using Justin as a tool to satisfy her own attention-seeking needs, causing harm to her child to fill whatever it was that was missing in her own life.

The nurses' station certainly wasn't the place to talk about it.

'Do you want me to do the oxygen saturations on the baby?' Rochelle offered as Eden rose to take Justin back to his cot. 'And then I can do the neuro obs.'

'I'll do the neuro obs,' Eden said, tactfully not adding that Nick would rather one of the more experienced staff members looked after his niece. Given the fact that he was the consultant on the ward, Eden could understand the unspoken request.

Never had she been more grateful for that split-second decision as she crept into the room to perform Harriet's neurological observations. A gnawing sense of foreboding niggled at her as she flicked on the overhead light and saw the awkward angle of her head on the pillow, but Eden didn't let it show. Instead, she smiled as an exhausted Lily stretched in the reclining chair by the bed and yawned a greeting.

'Hi, Lily,' Eden said. 'I'm just going to do Harriet's neuro obs and then I'll let you get back to sleep.' Gently she shook Harriet on the shoulder, calling her name a couple of times until Lily herself intervened, rousing her daughter from her deep sleep. 'Come on, honey,' Lily called. 'You remember Eden. She's just going to do your obs again. Remember how they shine that light in your eyes and you have to answer some questions?'

'Hi, Harriet,' Eden said softly as those familiar green eyes stared back at her. 'Do you remember me?'

A confused look flickered across the child's face and she shook her head slightly.

'It's the uniform,' Lily said firmly. 'Harriet, it's Eden. Remember she was with us for Christmas?'

'Do you know where you are, Harriet?' Eden asked, that niggling feeling increasing as the same confused eyes stared back at her.

'What's your name?' Eden asked, desperate to hear the little girl speak, her breath stuck in her throat until finally Harriet softly mouthed the word.

'She's tired,' Lily said quickly. 'She was at her father's all day. I think he took them to the beach. She'll be much brighter by the morning.'

'Harriet, can you squeeze my hands for me?' Eden said, placing her hands in the little girl's and feeling the pressure that she applied. 'Good,' she said, pulling back the sheet. 'Can you wiggle your toes for me? That's a good girl,' Eden encouraged her. 'Now, I want you to lift your legs up for me.' Putting her hand on Harriet's calf, she encouraged her further, noticing with growing disquiet that Harriet had already fallen back to sleep. 'Come on, Harriet, push my hand away.'

'She's exhausted,' Lily insisted. 'Look, I really think that she needs to sleep, Eden. I know you have to do these obs but surely, given that it's three a.m.…'

'I'm nearly finished,' Eden replied. 'I'm just going to shine a light in your eyes, Harriet, and then I'll let you rest.'

Shining the torch into Harriet's eyes, Eden didn't comment as Lily replaced the sheet around her daughter.

'Can I turn off the light?' Lily asked, and Eden nodded, slightly taken back by Lily's lack of concern.

'Sure,' Eden answered, frowning as she left the room and heading straight for the telephone. But even before she'd put out the page for Dr Timms's registrar, Nick was at the desk, obviously having set his watch alarm. He asked her how Harriet's obs had been.

'I'm just paging Dr Timms's registrar to discuss them,' Eden answered carefully, unsure how she should proceed, acutely aware that in this instance Nick was far from objective but wanting a doctor's opinion all the same.

'What's wrong Eden?' Nick's voice was not to be argued with. 'I'm not going to jump in with all guns blazing, I just need to know what's going on. Why are you paging the registrar? What's the problem with Harriet?'

'I'm not sure,' Eden admitted. 'I didn't actually see her on admission because she's Becky's patient, but she's at supper break now. I've just gone to do Harriet's two-hourly obs and…' Her voice trailed off, and she chewed her bottom lip as she attempted to voice her concern. 'On paper she seems fine, and admittedly it's the first time I've really seen her since she arrived from Emergency, but to me she seems altered.'

Nick gave her a worried look. 'Altered' was exactly that—an altered state of consciousness, a slight inappropriateness that wasn't always definable. 'She's answering questions, and she's obeying commands, but she just doesn't seem right. There's also a slight nystagmus.'

Nick's concerned frown deepened a fraction—nystagmus was a flickering of the eyes that was often a normal presentation in people but it could also indicate a neurological problem. 'I've had a quick look at the admission notes and it hasn't been recorded.'

'Because there wasn't one,' Nick said, dragging in a deep breath. 'What does Lily say?'

'I didn't mention the nystagmus to her but she didn't seem concerned at all. Lily seems to think that she's just tired. Perhaps she was the same on admission,' Eden offered, but privately she doubted it. Becky had given no indication of concern. 'Maybe I'm just overreacting.'

'I hope so,' Nick said. 'I'm going to check on her.'

'I'll come with you,' Eden said, calling Rochelle away from the saturations she was checking. 'Rochelle, I've just paged Dr Timms's registrar. When he calls back, can you ask him to come and review Harriet Mason?'

'What shall I say is wrong?'

'Just say that Dr Watson is in with Harriet now and that he'd like a doctor to come and assess her.' Eden called over her shoulder, and headed off to Harriet's room. But midway she halted, a gut feeling that couldn't be explained stopping her in her tracks. Heading back to the desk, she summoned Rochelle again.

'Go and knock on the staffroom door and ask Becky to come back from her break.'

'She's just gone back to sleep, Nick,' Lily was saying as Eden slipped into the room. 'Can't we just let her rest?'

'We need to check her,' Nick said firmly, running a careful eye over Harriet who was seemingly dozing on the bed.

But Eden just knew Nick was seeing the same as her, the awkward position that she was lying in, her head rotated awkwardly on the pillow. Lily was clearly less than impressed with the further intrusion and sucked in her breath, in irritation as Nick pulled back the sheet, gently rousing the little girl and noting her reaction to verbal stimulation.

'Hi, Harriet.' His voice was far less formal and he repeated the greeting a couple of times before gently shaking Harriet's shoulder.

'She's exhausted, Nick,' Lily argued, and Eden turned to the irritated woman, confused as to why, when Lily was a doctor herself, she would argue the point over something so that was obviously necessary. Then Eden realised that it was fear talking, that Lily quite simply didn't want to admit to the possibility that Harriet was really unwell. 'That's why she's not waking up—the poor kid is worn out.'

'Perhaps,' Eden conceded, 'and Nick will take into consideration the fact that Harriet is very tired, but it is imperative that he does a full examination on your daughter before we leave her to rest.'

A tiny nod from Lily indicated her consent and, knowing it was better for the young patient if her mother was included, Eden guided her closer to the bedside as Nick commenced his examination. Even though not by even a flicker did Nick betray his anxiety, as he moved the little girl's head to her chest Eden could tell that he was concerned. She'd worked alongside Nick for a long time now and could read from the tiny subtle shifts in his expressions, the way the lines that fanned around his eyes deepened, that Nick wasn't at all happy with what he was seeing.

'How are you feeling, Harriet?' He smiled down at his niece, who just stared back at him.

'Harriet, I need for you to talk to me. Are you sore anywhere?'

Again Harriet didn't answer, just stared back at her uncle with confused, anxious eyes.

'She answered you before?' Nick checked, and Eden gave a worried nod. 'Yes, well, when I say she answered, she just mouthed her name.'

'Harriet.' Lily's voice wobbled slightly. 'Answer Nick for me, honey.'

'Nick.' Something in Eden's voice dragged his attention away from the child. He watched where Eden's finger was pointing—a tiny red patch of skin no bigger than a pinhead with a small clear blister above it.

'That wasn't there before?' Nick asked, and there was definitely an urgent note to his voice now.

'No.' Eden shook her head. 'When I did her obs I checked for any rash. Let's sit you forward, Harriet,' she said immediately, not waiting for Nick, knowing he would want to examine Harriet's torso. 'There's another one,' she said, pointing to a small blister on her back as Nick looked behind Harriet's ears. 'And a few coming out here.'

'What going on?' Lily asked, staring at the faint rash on Harriet's body. 'What have you found…?' Her voice trailed off as she saw the emerging rash on her daughter, a hand smothering a sob as Nick flashed a torch in Harriet's eyes and repeated the reflex response check with a tendon hammer, gently reassuring the little girl when she let out a moan of protest.

'It's OK, Harriet, you can rest now. I'm just going to have a word with your mum and then I'll be back. Eden, can you get some acyclovir IV started?'

'She's got chickenpox, hasn't she?' Lily gulped. 'And if she's having this type of reaction it means that—'

'We'll talk outside,' Nick broke in quickly. Lily's tension could only upset Harriet further and Eden bit hard on her lip as he guided the frantic woman outside, pressing the buzzer on the wall three times in a code that told the ward that a member of staff required some rapid assistance. The emergency bell was only used when the situation was extremely serious.

'What's happening?' 'Rochelle asked.

'Have you called Becky?' Eden asked, barely able to disguise her irritation when Rochelle shook her head.

'I was on the phone with Dr Timms's reg. He's at home but he's going to come in soon.'

'What do you need?' Becky was back, summoned by the emergency bell and awake in a second.

'Her neuro obs are decreasing. Nick just examined her and it looks as if she's got chickenpox. Could you get me some acyclovir and a flask of saline? Nick will write it up when he gets back. And could you get the lab on the phone for Nick? He's going to want to speak to them.'

'Chickenpox?' Rochelle questioned, clearly bemused at her colleague's behaviour, but Eden didn't have the time to enlighten her. 'I'll explain later. Tell the switchboard to urgently page Dr Timms's registrar and let him know he needs to be here now!'

Even though it had only been fifteen minutes since Eden had done a set of observations she repeated the process, checking Harriet's vital signs. Though her pulse and blood pressure were relatively stable, Eden noted a marked decrease in her respiratory rate.

'Harriet!' Eden's voice was sharp, attempting to rouse the girl verbally. When the child responded to neither her voice nor a shoulder shake, she tweaked Harriet on her earlobe, calling her name in an urgent voice.

'Harriet!' Rubbing her sternum, Eden watched as Harriet's arms made only a small attempt to push her away, and Eden knew that her condition had deteriorated rapidly in just a few moments and that a rapid response was needed. Pushing the bell three times, she applied oxygen to the girl as Rochelle again dashed to the door.

'Get Nick—now!' Eden ordered. 'Actually…' She went over Harriet's symptoms in her head. Even though there was a consultant on the ward, Eden made a rapid decision. 'Get Nick in here and when you've done that call the medical emergency team and bring the crash trolley to the bedside,' she ordered, realising that the team needed to be summoned as in a matter of seconds Harriet could further deteriorate and require intubation.

'Shouldn't you run it by Nick?' Rochelle asked, but Eden flashed her a firm look. 'Just do it now, and get someone to stay with the mother.'

Attaching the oxygen saturation probe to Harriet she saw that despite the oxygen her saturation was only on ninety per cent, which was rather low. Flashing a torch into her eyes, Eden noted that her pupil responses were present but the little girl who had been talking only fifteen minutes ago, who had been celebrating Christmas and singing her heart out just a few days ago, was now slipping into unconsciousness. Eden felt her throat tighten as Harriet's body stiffened beneath her. The seizure she had anticipated had begun. Rolling Harriet swiftly onto her side, Eden willed the overhead chimes to go off, for help to arrive, relief flooding her when she heard Nick's footsteps and the door burst open as he rushed in.

'She just started seizing,' Eden explained. 'I've called a MET.' She held her breath for a second after she said it.

Rochelle hadn't been far off the mark when she'd queried whether Eden should run it by Nick first, given that he was on the ward. But Nick just gave a nod. He closed his eyes for a fraction of a second, as if willing his mind to clear, as if summoning the strength to push emotion aside and deal with this dire situation objectively. And even if she hated him for all he had done to her, Eden felt sorry for him now. To witness his own niece so desperately ill and to be the only doctor nearby would be a horrendous burden.

As the chimes went off overhead Becky arrived with the large red crash trolley, pulling up diazepam for Nick to give intravenously. But despite the drug, Harriet's seizure continued, and even though Eden knew the chimes that were ringing overhead were being played throughout the entire hospital, that at this very second the medical emergency team would be running towards the children's ward right now, the alarm on Harriet's oxygen saturation machine was going off too now. Her saturations were dangerously low and despite the diazepam, she continued to seize.

Rochelle was swinging into action now, moving chairs and tables out of the way to make room for the large trolley that was being wheeled in. And even though the emergency personnel were beginning to arrive, the situation was becoming more dire as Harriet's saturations dropped even lower. Nick started to pull off the bedhead and remove the pillows from under Harriet's head as Eden pulled open the intubation tray. She was grateful when the anaesthetist arrived. Nick at least would be spared from having to intubate his own niece.

'What's the story?' the anaesthetist asked, making straight to the head of the bed, assessing the situation with calm, knowing eyes and listening intently as Nick bought him up to speed.

'Five-year-old, admitted with first seizure. Neuro obs have rapidly deteriorated and we noted a classic chickenpox rash. She started seizing again.' Nick hesitated for a second. 'She's also my niece.'

'Should you be in here, then, Nick?' the anaesthetist asked, but didn't wait for an answer, his mind solely on the patient.

'How long has she been seizing now?' the anaesthetist asked, his finger probing the pulse in Harriet's neck then listening to her chest for air entry as Harriet's tiny body continued to convulse.

'Six minutes,' Eden responded, glancing down at her watch. 'She's had three lots of diazepam.'

'She can't keep on like this,' The anaesthetist was rummaging through the crash trolley, expertly pulling up the drugs of his choice. 'Let's paralyse and intubate. Sister, can I have some carotid pressure, please? Nick can you—?'

'I'll stay, thanks, Vince.' Nick's voice was calm and measured and completely in control but, glancing up briefly, Eden could see the sheer terror in his eyes and she was grateful when he stepped to the back of the room. He had realized that heroics weren't needed now, that the best he could do for his niece was stand back quietly and trust her life to his colleagues.

Eden's heart was in her mouth as Vince gently extended the little girl's neck. Eden applied the necessary pressure to allow the endotracheal tube to pass more easily and with her other hand passed him a laryngoscope, which allowed him to visualise the throat as he passed in the ET tube. His fingers snapped impatiently for Eden to pass the connections to the oxygen supply, waiting for the bag to inflate. It probably only took a couple of seconds but it felt like for ever.

'Has she had any acyclovir?' Vince asked, and Eden shook her head.

'We only just noticed the rash—'

'It's ready,' Becky broke in. 'It's all been checked.'

'Then let's get it started,' the anaesthetist said grimly. 'Can you ring ICU and let them know I'm bringing her straight up?' His foot was already kicking off the brake and Eden moved quickly, disconnecting the oxygen from the wall and attaching it to the portable cylinder, moving the monitors and dripstand onto the bed to prepare it for transfer as Becky dashed off to alert ICU.

'What's happening?' Dr Timms's registrar stood breathlessly at the door after a mad dash from the car park, his car keys jangling in his hand.

'I'll tell you on the way.'

'ICU wants ten minutes,' Becky called as she ran along the ward. Everywhere lights were flicking on, mothers alerted by the overhead chimes and commotion, babies abruptly woken from sleep crying for attention, but for now the sole concern was Harriet.

'ICU can keep on wanting,' Vince responded, continuing to move along the corridor and bagging Harriet as the rest of the MET staff pushed the bed, one running ahead to hold the lift doors open. 'This child doesn't have a spare ten minutes.' He glanced over at Nick, whose face was seemingly impassive, but Eden knew he was lacerated with pain. 'I'm sorry, Nick, I forgot you were here.'

'Just do what you can, Vince.' Nick's lips were white. 'Don't worry about me.'

Becky was grabbing Harriet's notes, running to catch up with the entourage, and Rochelle was wheeling the crash trolley back to the nurses' station. For a small slice of time, Eden and Nick were left alone, and for the first time in her life Eden truly didn't know what to say, didn't know how on earth to comfort him. Dragging her hair tie out, she ran a helpless hand through her hair and a tiny ghost of a smile dusted his taut lips at the familiar gesture.

'You don't have to say anything, Eden. This isn't anyone's fault.'

'I know that,' Eden choked. 'I just…' Helplessly she stood there, wanting so much to reach out and comfort him, to somehow convey that she felt his pain, but those days were long gone now. Her fists bunched at her sides as she struggled to keep her emotions in check. 'I'd better tell Lily what's going on.'

'I already know.' A tiny figure emerged from

the darkness, fear, pain and grief etched on every feature. Nick was on the ball because just as Lily's knees buckled he caught her. Strong arms wrapping around his sister, he guided her down the long lonely walk to ICU and all Eden could do was stand there and watch them leave.

CHAPTER ELEVEN

'BUT how?' For what seemed the hundredth time Rochelle voiced the question that no one could really answer as Eden struggled to feed a restless Ben.

The ward had long since been cleaned up, the crash trolley restocked. In theory Eden could probably have gone for her break, but sitting down and flicking through a magazine held no particular charm right now so instead she was attempting to settle Ben, who no doubt was picking up on Eden's heart still thumping in her chest and refusing to take his bottle. Rochelle stood at Ben's doorway, clearly stunned at the rapid turn of events and desperately needing to talk.

'I mean, the poor kid's only got chickenpox!'

'It's very common.' Eden nodded. 'Unfortunately, in some cases the side effects can be severe.'

'But it all happened so quickly,' Rochelle said.

'That's the way it is with children,' Eden explained. 'They can hold their vital signs for a long time, appear relatively well, but when their condition deteriorates it can be extremely rapid. That's why we do such frequent observations on the children's ward—they can't always tell you themselves that they're not feeling well.'

'If I'd done Harriet's obs, would I have picked it up? I mean, his mum's a doctor and she didn't seem concerned. What chance would I have had?'

'I don't know,' Eden admitted, 'but I can guarantee that next time you do a set of neuro obs and every time for the rest of your nursing career, you'll remember what just happened and be on the lookout for anything that doesn't seem quite right.'

'He's nearly asleep,' Rochelle observed, smiling from the doorway at Ben. 'He likes it when you're talking.'

'He does,' Eden said fondly gazing down at a now relaxed Ben. His eyes were closed and he was sucking hard on his bottle. She took the opportunity to explain in a bit more detail what had just happened to Harriet.

'As I said, chickenpox can have some quite nasty side effects, one of them being viral encephalitis, which means an inflammation of the brain. Now, in Harriet's case, the inflammation caused the seizure that brought her to Emergency. Often, first seizures are sent home and followed up with outpatient appointments, but because Harriet was febrile it was decided to keep her in hospital for observation.'

'But she didn't even have a rash.'

'She didn't have to,' Eden patiently explained. 'The fact she was febrile and had had a seizure indicated there was some type of infection going on. It could have been nothing more than a mild ear infection, but until a diagnosis was made no one could be sure. At the back of the doctor's mind would have been the possibility if not of viral encephalitis then certainly meningitis—that's why she was kept in isolation until we knew exactly what was going on.'

'But will she be OK?'

And that was the one question, as much as she wanted to, Eden couldn't really answer.

'I don't know, Rochelle,' Eden admitted. 'They've started her on some strong antiviral medication and they'll probably give her some steroids to reduce the inflammation to her brain, but it really is going to be a case of wait and see.'

'Could she have brain damage?' Rochelle asked, and even though her question was merited, Eden closed her eyes in horror, scarcely able to comprehend herself that the vibrant beautiful girl she had shared Christmas with now lay in Intensive Care in a critical condition.

'She might,' Eden said softly. 'But there's one good thing about working with children. As quickly as they decline, they also pick up very rapidly. Let's just hope that's the case with Harriet.'

But despite her confident words, despite the hope she tried to imbue, as the night progressed, as notes were written and the morning round commenced, the horror of what had taken place never left her mind. Her heart ached for Lily and what she must be going through, and even though she was loathe to admit it, even to herself, she felt desperate for Nick, for all he had been through and for all he was suffering now.

When handover had been given and the day staff had been bought up to date with the night's events, Eden pulled on her jacket and slipped into Ben's room for a quick goodbye. She knew she had to go up and check on Harriet's progress before she left the hospital.

She knew that, despite her own pain, she couldn't walk away without letting Nick know she was thinking of him.

Bracing herself, Eden entered Intensive Care. Introducing herself to the nurse in charge and checking it was OK, she made her way over to Harriet's cubicle, standing quietly outside the glass window and staring in.

'How is she?' Eden asked as Lavinia, one of the charge nurses she vaguely knew, came up beside her.

'About as sick as a five-year-old can be. The mother's just gone to ring the father. Apparently they're separated. Imagine the poor guy when he picks up the phone and hears this news.'

'How's Nick?' Eden asked, already knowing the answer.

'Beside himself, of course. He thinks that he should somehow have worked out what was wrong sooner. He's berating himself that the acyclovir wasn't started down in Emergency. As if, I told him, we're going to start acyclovir on every febrile child that comes into the hospital.'

'He's just scared, I guess,' Eden said, staring through the glass at Nick. Draped in a white gown and even with a mask covering his face, the raw anguish was visible in his eyes and all she could do was repeat Rochelle's words.

'The poor kid's only got chickenpox.'

* * *

The worst thing about night shift was Eden's total inability to sleep during the day, and that morning was no exception. Lying on her back, she stared wide-eyed at the ceiling, going over and over in her head the previous night's events, wondering over and over if something—anything—could have been done that might somehow have changed the outcome.

'Oh, Nick.' The words shivered on her lips, the face that had haunted her for days swimming into focus every time she closed her eyes. Even though she was still reeling from his callous rejection, she was completely unable to hate him. Her mind was a horrible jumbled mess. She was furious with herself for crying over someone she didn't mean a thing to yet unable to stop.

Giving in, Eden padded into the kitchen. The house was impossibly quiet without Jim. She dropped two pieces of bread into the toaster and pulled some margarine and Vegemite out of the fridge, comfort food definitely the order of the day! There was something infinitely comforting about tea and toast in bed. She stared unseeing at a midmorning chat show on her faithful portable TV, watching as a relationship guru shared his wisdom, listening to the appalling mess people made of their lives and realising she'd done exactly the same.

Becky was wrong, Eden decided, her mind finally made up. Placing her plate on the bedside table and flicking off the television, she shut down other people's problems and for once really concentrated on her own.

The hardest thing wasn't walking away, it was staying to watch love die.

Her mind made up, Eden closed her eyes.

The first real sleep she'd had since Boxing Day finally washed over her.

CHAPTER TWELVE

'Is this about Ben?' Donna stared at the sheet of paper in front of her, rereading the neat hand-writing once again before looking over to where Eden sat at the other side of the desk.

'In part,' Eden admitted. 'But there are other factors involved.'

'Are you going to enlighten me?' Donna asked, frowning as Eden shook her head. 'You're not giving the ward much notice, Eden.'

'I've got a week off after tonight,' Eden pointed out. 'And after that I've still got four weeks' annual leave owing. I know it might be difficult to fill the roster, but—'

'I'm not worried about the roster,' Donna broke in. 'I'm worried about you, Eden. I can fill a few shifts, but I can't replace a dedicated, knowledgeable paediatric nurse so easily. I thought you were happy here.'

'I am,' Eden answered, desperately trying to keep her voice even, to keep her emotions in check and just make it through this awkward interview. 'Or, rather, I have been. I just think I need a change.'

'And you have to leave tonight?' Donna frowned. 'On New Year's Eve?'

'I know it's a lot to ask—but I just want a fresh start.' Eden swallowed. 'I saw a position advertised in the intensive care unit at the children's hospital. I want a fresh challenge.'

'You're sure?' Donna checked. 'There's nothing I can say to make you change your mind?'

'Nothing,' Eden gulped, and she braced for the protest, for Donna to dig deeper, to try to get to the bottom of things. Instead, she was standing up and offering her hand, which almost reluctantly Eden took.

'Then I wish you well, Sister. I'll be happy to provide a reference for you.'

'I'm sorry if I'm leaving you short,' Eden attempted, slightly taken back by the ease in which Donna had accepted the news.

'We'll manage.' Donna smiled. 'I need nurses who want to be here, Eden.'

'I know.' Eden nodded.

'You haven't exactly given us time to arrange a leaving do or a collection—'

'I don't want anything,' Eden broke in. 'I just want to slip away.'

'Run away perhaps?' Donna said, raising an eyebrow, but when Eden didn't react instead she offered her hand. 'Good luck, Eden.'

And that, Eden realised, as she shakily made her way into her last handover, was that. No fanfares, no tearful goodbyes. She could walk away with her head held high.

So why didn't it feel good?

'I don't believe her,' Becky huffed as Donna marched off the ward without even stopping to say goodbye. 'It's New Year's Eve, for good-ness' sake, and she expects us to take the Christmas decorations down.'

'Well, we're not,' Eden said. Becky had, no

doubt, been expecting a small murmur of protest, but there was a definite note of defiance in Eden's voice that had Nick, who was on the phone, looking up. 'It's still Christmas. Decorations aren't supposed to be taken down until Twelfth Night, which isn't until the sixth of January.'

'Try telling that to Donna,' Becky said, rolling her eyes.

'I will,' Eden responded. 'There's no way I'm taking them down. It's bad luck.'

'Actually,' Nick corrected her, covering the mouthpiece with his hand 'it's bad luck to leave them up after the sixth.'

'Same thing,' Eden retorted.

'Hey, I'm on your side,' Nick sighed, putting down the phone. 'Frankly, I could use all the luck I can get tonight. They're going to extubate Harriet.'

'I heard,' Eden said. 'She seems to be responding well to treatment.'

Nick gave a very tentative nod. 'We'll know more once they take the tube out. There's still a long way to go, but at least she's fighting. I'll be in Intensive Care if you need me.'

'We won't,' Becky responded. 'For once the ward's just about empty and I, for one, intend to make the most of it. We deserve a quiet night after the last few we've had.'

'Well, I'm off,' Nick answered, clicking off his pen and placing it in his top suit pocket. For an indulgent moment Eden stared, capturing this moment, tracing his features with her eyes, trying to somehow etch them on her mind, knowing that it might be the last time she saw him. 'And don't you dare take down those decorations. Happy New Year, ladies.'

'Happy New Year, Nick,' Becky said. 'We'll ring Intensive Care later and see how Harriet is. Good luck!'

Maybe he felt the weight of her stare, maybe he sensed there was something going on, but Nick stared at Eden for a long moment, frowning slightly at her pensive face.

'Good luck with Harriet,' Eden croaked.

'Thanks, Eden...' Still he stood there and Eden was sure there was something he was about to say, but whatever it was he chose otherwise, giving her the briefest of nods and heading off to Intensive Care.

Ben seemed to know something was up and refused to go to sleep, giggling and waving every time Eden walked past the room. When he didn't know she was watching he played peek-a-boo with the mirror that was attached to his cot, the absolute cutest he had ever been, as if making some last-ditch effort to win her heart.

'*Den,*' he squealed when she finally came into the room and pulled on her gown, going through the familiar routine of changing his nappy before feeding him, catching legs that were kicking their protest and dressing him in his new pyjamas, brushing his teeth for him. Finally, when all the chores were done, she cuddled him close and gave him his bottle.

'You're going to be fine,' Eden said firmly, as if to convince herself. 'Donna was telling me this evening that Lorna's found a wonderful new home for you. There will be lots of other children there, lots of friends to play with.'

Tears that couldn't fall tonight threatened to choke her, a residential unit the very last thing she had wanted for Ben. If Eden hadn't been sure, she knew then she was making the right decision. She couldn't bear the thought of seeing Ben when, as was inevitable with his condition, he was readmitted, knowing that the one thing the little guy really deserved, really needed, was going to be denied.

That he'd never have a family.

'Fifteen minutes till midnight,' Becky said as Eden came and sat down, taking a grateful drink of the coffee Becky had made her. 'And the Christmas tree lights are still on. We're going to be in trouble in the morning.'

'We'd better take them down before the morning,' Eden sighed.

'What happened to your sudden streak of assertiveness?' Becky grinned.

'It scared the life out of me. You know how useless I am at saying no. Do you mind if I take first break?' Eden asked. 'I might head up to the roof and watch the fireworks over the harbour.'

'Go for it,' Becky said, then screwed up her

nose. 'Bloody fireworks. I refuse to watch them on principle. Imagine burning thousands of dollars that could be spent providing meals for some poverty-stricken country.'

The diamond rocks in Becky's ears would provide a whole new irrigation system, Eden felt like pointing out, but realised her bad mood wasn't Becky's fault. Eden didn't say anything, just pulled on her cardigan and headed out of the ward, taking a moment to stop and stare at Ben, who was finally asleep, the sheet she had tucked around him discarded on the floor, his little bottom sticking up in the air, thumb firmly in mouth. Eden thought her heart would break.

The roof of the hospital was a fairly open secret and Eden half expected to find a crowd gathered there to watch the New Year firework display, but clearly the other wards weren't as quiet as the paediatric unit tonight and Eden stood alone, staring out to Sydney Harbour, seeing the elegant shape of the Opera House and the impressive sight of the Sydney Harbour Bridge. Hundreds of boats were out on the water in prime vantage points. Despite the warm night air, Eden shivered, pulling her cardigan tighter around her, jumping when she heard footsteps coming up behind her. Even before she turned Eden knew it was Nick.

'How is she?' Eden asked, and for a moment she thought the news must be bad when she saw the sparkle of tears in his eyes, the sheer tension in his face. But he gave a small hesitant nod, even managed a smile.

'So far so good.' His voice was thick with emotion. 'There's still a hell of a long way to go, but her eyes are open, she's moving her arms and legs and she recognises us all.'

'Thank God,' Eden whispered, and Nick nodded.

'I really thought we were going to lose her, Eden. When you think how bad it could have been, this really is a Christmas miracle.'

Eden didn't answer, just stared out into the night sky, waiting for the firework display to start, praying for this year to be over so she could get on with her life, yet terrified all the same, wondering how her life would be this time next year.

'You're leaving, aren't you?' His question was direct and Eden stiffened beside him.

Her first reaction was to deny it but, a useless liar at the best of times, finally she gave a short nod. 'I asked Donna not to say anything.'

'She didn't,' Nick answered. 'I just guessed.'

'How?'

'I was watching you work earlier. I don't know, something told me you were preparing to leave.' He hesitated for the longest time. 'Is it because of what happened between us?'

'It's because of a lot of things,'

'Ben?' Nick asked, and Eden nodded.

'I know now why we're not supposed to get involved. It isn't just for the patient's protection, it's for us as well.'

'You can still see him, Eden,' Nick pointed out. 'You can provide respite care, take him out for a day, even if he is in a children's home.'

'It isn't enough,' Eden choked. 'I thought it would be, thought if I could just have a little piece of him, make him happy some of the time, then that would make things better. But it hasn't and I just can't do it any more. I think it would be easier for me if I didn't see him at all.'

And for a second there Eden truly didn't know if she was talking about Ben or Nick, her agony blurring things into one painful mass.

'When do you leave?' Nick asked, his voice tentative, and Eden saw a flicker of regret in his eyes when she answered.

'This is my last night Nick.'

'No.' Fiercely he shook his head. 'Eden, don't go, not like this…'

A massive crash in the distance ended his protest as the whole night sky lit up in a glorious display of colour. They stood watching the new year come in, the spectacular fireworks in the distance lighting up Sydney Harbour, the joyous sounds of revellers in the streets below. And even though there was plenty to focus on, she was achingly aware of Nick beside her, and the fact that she didn't know what to say or what to do. As hard as leaving was, staying would be torture—seeing him every day and knowing she couldn't have him, living on the pathetic hope of an occasional drink or—who knew?—perhaps the odd night together when Nick was feeling lonely and she didn't have the power to say no. A final fanfare of green and gold sparkled to the heavens, the bridge emblazoned with the numbers of the new year that would be forever etched on her heart. A year of new beginnings, but right now she had to get through the painful ending. She turned to him and offered a tremulous smile for her own inadequate words as she wished Nick well.

'I hope…'

'Hope what, Eden?'

'That this year's kinder for you.'

And a New Year's kiss was appropriate, a kiss goodbye, letting go all that could have been. But even as his lips dusted hers, Eden felt the shameful response of her body. Her own hands reached for him and she lost herself in that kiss, offering comfort. He drank it from her, the pent-up misery, the utter wretchedness of the past few weeks were momentarily suspended.

'Don't go, Eden.'

'I have to,' Eden said finally. 'Because this isn't fair on me, Nick. And I'm sorry if I can't be what you want, sorry that I can't just be a casual date or even a friend or colleague, because I just wasn't made that way. All I want to do, all I've ever wanted to do, is love you. And I'm not proud of that, especially as for some of the time you were engaged to Teaghan. I know you'll never feel for me a tenth of what you felt for her, but what you did to me the other night was cruel in the extreme. Nick, you used me and then you pushed me away, made something that was so right suddenly dirty and cheap, made me feel guilty for even caring about you. And I just can't get past that, Nick. I can't pretend that I'm OK with it for even a moment longer. I'm not going to let you use me the same way you used Tanya and countless others. I'm not going to be one of your diversions just so that you can deaden the pain of losing Teaghan.'

Pushing him away, she headed for the stairwell, appalled at what she had just admitted, that again she'd revealed the depths of her feelings to a man who simply didn't know how to love. But she was relieved, too, relieved that finally she'd admitted the truth.

'Eden.' She could hear him calling, but she chose to ignore him, pressing furiously on the lift button and jumping inside when it opened. She let out a sigh of relief as the doors closed and the lift descended. She rapidly made her way back to the safety of the children's ward, knowing Nick couldn't confront her there. Ben was still asleep and Becky exactly where she'd left her, except for the addition of a radio playing softly at the desk, a pile of notes waiting to be written—the whole world just moving right along.

CHAPTER THIRTEEN

'CAN I have a word, Eden?' Nick's voice was sharp, but Eden didn't look up. She'd already said more than she'd intended, already boosted his already over-inflated ego a touch further but, more importantly, Eden knew she couldn't carry on the conversation without breaking down and was determined to leave with what was left of her dignity intact. 'Eden,' Nick snapped, but still she ignored him, picking up a pen and grabbing a pile of obs charts.

'Where are you up to, Becky?'

'Room four,' Becky answered nervously, her eyes swinging from Nick to Eden. 'But I can do the charts if Nick needs to talk to you.'

'He doesn't,' Eden said through gritted teeth, grabbing a ruler and drawing an angry red line through the chart on the desk in front of her, wishing he would just go away and leave her to die in peace!

'Oh, but he does,' Nick responded, and from his tone Eden knew there was no arguing with him, that if she didn't go into his office the whole ward was about to become privy to her private pain. 'We can either go into my office, Eden, or I'll say what I have to say here. What's it to be?'

Becky and Rochelle sat up straighter, visibly perking up at the prospect of front-row seats. Even a tired-looking mum walking past the nurses' station with her baby's bottle in her hand paused at the desk, pretending to need a tissue.

'I won't be long, Becky,' Eden bristled, standing up. 'Two minutes at the most.'

In a final stab at assertion Eden refused to follow him, marching angrily ahead and flinging open *his* office door, turning angrily to face him as Nick closed it behind him.

'How dare you embarrass me like that in front of my colleagues?'

'How dare you say what you did and then walk away?' Nick's face was taut, his lips set in a grim line, but Eden refused to back down.

'I'm only speaking the truth, Nick. It's not my fault if you don't like it.'

'You don't know the truth,' Nick barked, an angry muscle leaping on his cheek. Every muscle in his body seemed coiled like a spring and Eden jumped back. In all the time she'd known him, not once had she seen him angry, not once had she seen him anything other than relaxed and in control. 'And you don't know the first thing about guilt either!' Anguished eyes held hers, pain she had never before witnessed, even when she'd broken the tragic news of what had happened to Teaghan, was there now for her to see.

'What have you got to feel guilty about, Nick?' Eden asked, but her voice was softer now. 'It was an accident…'

'We were breaking up when it happened,' Nick rasped. 'Or, rather, I'd just broken things off.'

'I'm sorry.' Eden closed her eyes in regret for him. 'But it doesn't mean that it was your fault.'

'Do you know what her last words were to me?' Nick asked, and Eden shook her head. '"Your *girlfriend* is on duty this morning, Nick, you don't have to deny it any more!" That was the last thing she said to me, Eden. She stormed out of here, full of rage and bitterness. It's no wonder she wasn't concentrating on the road.'

'Nick.' Again Eden shook her head, struggling to say the right thing. 'It still doesn't mean it was your fault. Couples break up—'

'It was over you, Eden!' Her mouth snapped closed as Nick overrode her. 'As soon as you started working here, Teaghan got it into her head that I liked you. We'd been having problems for ages, we'd nearly broken up the Christmas before, but this thing between you and I brought it to a head.'

'But there wasn't anything going on between us,' Eden whispered, her own face pale now, finally understanding Nick's guilt because her own was starting to trickle in. When Nick slowly shook his head, looked into her eyes and willed her to admit the truth, the dam burst, the trickle turning into a torrent as the truth was finally out.

'Yes, Eden, there was,' Nick said slowly. 'As much as I denied it to Teaghan, as much as I refused to admit it to myself, I did have feelings for you.

'I always have.' Nick's own eyes were swimming with tears now. 'And I always will, Eden. That night when you were upset about Ben, I was out of my mind with jealousy. I didn't want it to be Jim cheering you up, Jim going for pizza and trying to comfort you—I wanted it to be me.'

'I wanted it to be you, too,' Eden admitted. 'I just didn't want to risk getting hurt, didn't want to be another woman hanging onto your every word.'

'You're wrong about what you said about Tanya. I haven't slept with anyone except you since Teaghan died.' He registered her slightly incredulous look. 'I haven't,' he insisted. 'Sure, I've tried dating a few times, but I've always made it clear from the start I didn't want a relationship. But no matter how much I tried to deny it, no matter how much I wanted to somehow prove Teaghan wrong, I *did* want a relationship. And the only person I wanted to be with was you.'

'You told me that on Christmas night, Nick,' Eden pointed out, 'but it didn't stop you from tossing me aside the next day.'

'Her parents rang.' His voice was so low she had to strain to catch it. 'They wanted to know if I was coming to the cemetery with them, and all I could think was that you were lying in my bed, that Teaghan had been right about it all along. That I betrayed her because I'd always wanted you.'

She saw it from his side then, glimpsed the great abyss of his grief—meaningless attempts at relationships in an effort to run from the truth, trying to deny feelings that had always been there.

Always been there.

'You didn't kill her, Nick.' Her voice was amazingly calm. 'And neither did I. We've done nothing wrong.'

'Then why doesn't it feel that way?' Nick asked. 'Why do I feel so guilty for loving you?'

Which was a big difference from wanting. Eden's breath caught in her throat as the true depth of his feelings were revealed.

'I love you, Eden.' Crossing the room, he wrapped his arms tightly around her and buried his face in her hair, dragging in her scent, holding onto her as if he couldn't bear to ever let her go. 'I love you,' he said again, but more forcefully this time, as if shutting out the demons that had haunted him. Pulling away slightly, he stared down at her, captured her face in her hands and said it all over again, without shame or regret now, a burden lifted for ever as the simple truth was revealed.

'I love you, too,' Eden whispered. 'Always have and always will.' A terrible thought suddenly occurred to her, her forehead creasing as Nick smiled down at her. 'I've just handed in my notice!'

'Good.' Nick said, raining butterfly kisses on her face as she nervously chewed her bottom lip.

'It isn't good,' she protested.

'Oh, but it is,' Nick said. 'You can apply for your job all over again tomorrow. Donna will take you back, but you can tell her that you'll only accept under certain conditions.'

'Which are?'

'Absolutely no night duty,' Nick said, 'and next year you have all of Christmas off.'

'Fat chance,' Eden mumbled, but, given it was only the first of January, she didn't really care, and there was a whole delicious twelve months to fill in between now and then.

'You won't be working, Eden,' Nick said firmly. 'This time next year you'll be taking care of a family of your own.'

EPILOGUE

'YOU'RE DOING TOO much.'

Seeing Eden standing in her uniform, pulling a hastily prepared casserole out of the oven, Nick dropped his briefcase on the floor. Crossing the kitchen, he kissed her full on the lips before resuming his protest.

'Eden, I thought we'd agreed no night shifts. You're looking really tired.'

'I know,' Eden admitted. 'But it isn't the odd night shift that's making me tired…'

'The whole point of you working for the hospital bank,' Nick broke in, 'is so that you can pick and choose your shifts!'

'The ward is really short,' Eden said, buttering jacket potatoes and scooping the casserole over them. 'It's only for one night.'

'That's what you said last week,' Nick reminded her, grabbing a spoon from the drawer and scraping the dish. 'And the week before. When are you going to start saying no?'

'You didn't mind my inability to say no last night.' Eden cheekily grinned. 'Anyway, one night a week isn't going to kill me.'

But Nick just rolled his eyes. 'Well it's sure as hell going to finish me off. Have you any idea how much this one plays up once you've gone to work?'

'Then don't wake him,' Eden answered. 'There's no need to check on him five minutes after I leave the house.'

As if on cue, the sound of footsteps running along the hallway had them both turning and watching as an elated Ben scampered towards them, clearly delighted at the sound of Nick's voice.

'Home!' he squealed as Nick scooped him up and showered him with kisses.

'Yep, buddy, I'm home!'

Home was Ben's favourite new word! In the six months since they'd become permanent foster-parents, Ben said it a thousand times a day. *Home* as the car rounded the corner and their weatherboard house came into view, *home* whenever Nick came in at night or Eden arrived back in the morning, the single word making him smile each and every time it spilled from his smiling chubby face.

'Donna was saying that the Christmas roster is already done. She wanted to know if I wanted any shifts.'

'I hope you told her no!' Nick said with a note of alarm. 'This will be our first Christmas as a family so no way are you working a single shift in December—or January either, come to that.'

'I'm not,' Eden said, placing the plates on the table and helping Ben into his seat as Nick cut up the little boy's dinner. 'And I won't be working next Christmas either,' Eden added, holding her breath, waiting for Nick to look up. But he was tucking into the rather burnt casserole and trying to feed Ben at the same time.

'Good,' Nick said, totally missing the point.

'You know I went to see the doctor today,' Eden started, finally catching his attention.

'I meant to ring you about that. I asked the GP to fax Ben's bloods over to me when they came back. Well, I spoke to the ID consultant about them and he's thrilled. He says that Ben couldn't be doing any better—'

'The GP told me,' Eden broke in, wondering why on the films it always looked so easy, how with one tiny shift of the head the penny would suddenly drop. A sledgehammer would be the only thing that would get Nick's full attention tonight! 'I won't be working next Christmas because—'

When Nick's pager chose that moment to go off, Eden thought she might burst with frustration as he headed off to the phone to ring the hospital.

'Nick, I'm trying to talk to you.'

'I'll just be a moment.' Picking up the phone, he flashed an apologetic smile, punched in the hospital's number and introduced himself to the switchboard operator. All Eden knew was that she had to say it now or he'd be on the phone for hours!

'I'm pregnant, Nick!'

He stopped dead. His whole body went stock still. Only his eyes moved taking in her nervous, excited face, a slow, incredulous smile breaking out on his face as he digested the news. Suddenly remembering he was on the phone, he apologised to the switchboard operator, saying that he'd call back.

'Thanks very much!' he said, replacing the receiver and crossing the room. 'Switchboard sends congratulations! How long have you known?' he went on.

Eden glanced at the oven clock. 'Three hours and five minutes.'

'And you didn't tell me.' Nick grinned, but there were tears sparkling in his expressive eyes.

'I've been trying to,' Eden said. 'Since the second you got home. *That's* why I'm looking so tired, *that's* why I went to the doctor and *that's* why I won't be working next Christmas—because it will be our baby's first one!'

'You're not working tonight either,' Nick said, refusing to budge as Eden begged to differ. 'No way,' Nick said. 'You, Eden Watson, are going to learn how to say no! I want you here at home tonight—both of you,' he added, his hand brushing her stomach. She captured it, holding it there and revelling in its warmth.

'Home!' Ben repeated loudly, making them both jump—his little face filthy from five minutes' neglect, smothered in chicken casserole, his hair matted with jacket potato.

'Home,' Nick agreed, kissing her deeply before continuing. 'With your family.'

MEDICAL ROMANCE™

—⩗— *Large Print* —⩗—

Titles for the next three months...

July

HER CELEBRITY SURGEON	Kate Hardy
COMING BACK FOR HIS BRIDE	Abigail Gordon
THE NURSE'S SECRET SON	Amy Andrews
THE SURGEON'S RESCUE MISSION	Dianne Drake

August

NEEDED: FULL-TIME FATHER	Carol Marinelli
THE SURGEON'S ENGAGEMENT WISH	Alison Roberts
SHEIKH SURGEON	Meredith Webber
THE EMERGENCY DOCTOR'S PROPOSAL	Joanna Neil
TELL ME YOU LOVE ME	Gill Sanderson
THE DOCTOR'S COURAGEOUS BRIDE	Dianne Drake

September

HIS SECRET LOVE-CHILD	Marion Lennox
HER HONOURABLE PLAYBOY	Kate Hardy
THE SURGEON'S PREGNANCY SURPRISE	Laura MacDonald
IN HIS LOVING CARE	Jennifer Taylor
HIGH-ALTITUDE DOCTOR	Sarah Morgan
A FRENCH DOCTOR AT ABBEYFIELDS	Abigail Gordon

MILLS & BOON®

Live the emotion

0606 LP 1P Medical